BEES
ON THE
ROOF

For further information, contact:
Tumblehome Learning, Inc.
201 Newbury St, Suite 201
Boston, MA 02116
http://www.tumblehomelearning.com

Library of Congress Control Number 2018936361

ISBN 978-1-943431-24-3

Shell, Robbie
Bees on the Roof / Robbie Shell - 2nd ed

Cover Art - Anna Heigh

Printed in the United States of America

10 9 8 7 6 5 4 3 2 1

BEES
ON THE
ROOF

By
Robbie Shell

TUMBLEHOME l e a r n i n g, Inc.

Dedication

To Honeybees and Beekeepers Everywhere

CONTENTS

Chapter 1

Let the Competition Begin

Sam looked into the mirrored wall of the elevator as it sped nonstop from the fifteenth floor to the hotel's kitchen. The tuft of sandy brown hair that usually hung down almost to his eyes was in disarray despite the gel he had rubbed in five minutes earlier. Two cowlicks remained defiant, standing straight up, as if a small whiskbroom had taken root on his head while he slept.

Six thirty a.m. It was still dark outside, and the backpack that hung heavily off his shoulder felt like someone had secretly filled it with twenty pounds of wet sand.

He knew his father had already been awake for an hour overseeing three assistant pastry chefs as they began to whip huge vats of cream, beat dozens of eggs, and do the prep work for dough, batters, icings, and fillings. That was just for starters. The Meadows hotel and its four-star Bella Vista restaurant were catering a post-holiday afternoon party, and the centerpiece was going to be a huge cake in the shape of a Porsche racing car, its sleek body covered with silver icing anchored by chocolate wheels.

Sam navigated his way through the countertops to a small table at the back. He reached into one of the aluminum refrigerators for milk and juice, poured himself a bowl of cereal, and thought about the day ahead—January 2, the beginning of the long, cold, post-holiday slog. It was hard to believe that he was already halfway through seventh grade, still harder to believe that it was six months since his father had been hired at the high end Bella Vista in midtown Manhattan and given, along with the title of head pastry chef, the use of a two-bedroom apartment at the top of the hotel.

"Bye, Dad," he shouted to Nick, jumping up from the table and knocking over a milk carton as he bolted for the service door leading out to the street. Uh-oh, I'm in for it now, he thought. Time for the lecture on slowing down, watching what I'm doing, never assuming that other people will clean up after me. "Dad, I'm sorry about the milk." Sam went over to the table where his father was preparing a small bowl of orange frosting for the Porsche's racing stripes. "I'll wash the floor when I get home." An easy promise. No way the staff was going to let a puddle of milk sit there all day.

His father stared, one eyebrow raised, at the mess. "Sam, we'll take care of it, just this once. You can't afford to be late to school—again. Remember your New Year's resolution."

You mean *your* resolution, Sam thought, pulling his New York Mets cap out of his backpack while Nick launched into one of those thankfully short, man-to-man speeches: "Okay, son, this is an important day, the start of the second half of the school year. It's going to be getting harder and harder, but I know that you will do well, like always, and I am so proud of you, and get going so you won't be late, and I love you," or something like that. The ritual hug, and Sam was out the door, chocolate chip muffin in one hand and metro pass in the other. With luck, the subways would be running on schedule, and he could slide into school, barely awake but on time.

****

Matt, Ella, and Tristan were waiting for him outside the main auditorium of the Manhattan School for Science, the private and very prestigious midtown school for grades seven through twelve. January's opening assembly was scheduled to start in five minutes, and eighty seventh graders were heading for their reserved section in the back.

"This is going to be a long three-and-a-half months—no real break until spring vacation, more papers, more labs, more group assignments. Wake me up when it's April," Sam whispered to his friends. They found their seats, so far off to the side that Sam was sure no teacher would see his eyes close, his head droop ever so slightly onto his chest. He dimly heard the principal's droning reference to "the always brilliant, always mind-bending ideas that our seventh graders come up with for the science competition."

Then she went off script. "This year, for the first time, the winning team is being invited to Washington, D.C., for an event sponsored by the National Science Foundation that will give awards to the best projects in ten different categories."

Sam felt the back rows of the assembly suddenly jolt awake, as if an invisible rope had pulled their spines straight up out of the usual morning-assembly slouch. "That means you will be competing against winners from other seventh grades around the country," the principal said. "But win or lose, our team will be the NSF's guests for a three-day weekend that will include a visit to Capitol Hill, the Supreme Court building, the Air and Space Museum, *and* a meeting at the White House with the President of the United States!"

There was more. In another first, the principal announced that the competition this year would continue through the summer rather than end in late May, with the winners to be chosen at the beginning of school in September. "During the spring, you will have time to dive into your chosen projects and then present a comprehensive progress report to your faculty science advisor by the end of school in June. At that point, we will choose eight projects out of the twenty that we feel are showing exceptional promise, and those eight teams will have the option of using the summer months to continue their explorations."

She raised her arm in a slightly awkward rallying cry: "Let the competition begin!"

The science project. Sam had forgotten about that, but now a few sentences from the seventh grade syllabus slowly resurfaced: Students were instructed to divide themselves into four-member teams, choose a topic, and do all sorts of research using whatever resources in whatever formats they could find. He remembered one particular phrase in the syllabus because it sounded so *adult*: Students would be judged on "how convincingly they show the relevance of their topic to the world beyond the classroom."

"Good sell, I mean about the science project," Tristan said to Sam as they left the auditorium with Matt and Ella. "But it'll be hard to keep up the excitement. I mean it's only January. Winners won't be chosen for nine months."

Ella pointed to four students clustered into a tight circle off to the side, their voices low, their heads bent forward as if they were plotting revenge on an overly demanding gym teacher. "I don't think that's going to be a problem," she said. "The human wrecking ball coming our way will make sure no one forgets there's a contest with a winner-take-all prize at the end."

Sam watched Reed, followed by his gang of three, promenading down the hall towards him. He looked especially giraffe-like today, with his elongated, slightly arced neck and small, flat ears pinned onto his head like crooked commas. All that's missing, Sam thought, are the two "horns"—actually, bony knobs that grow out of a giraffe's skull and are used to woo mating partners. How appropriate.

Reed stopped, taking in Sam and Tristan and lingering for a moment on Ella. "Hey, guys," Reed smirked. "Good luck on the science project. As if you stand a chance."

He swiveled his neck around to look at Matt. "You know what we have going for us? The fact that you're not on our team. Any idiot can predict how this is going to end." His parting words shot out like little bullets: "Washington. D.C. Here. We. Come."

He sauntered off trailed by his friends—short, squat Miles; Charlene, her oblong gold earrings swinging like tiny nooses; and finally Jeremy, so thin and pale that from the side he looked like a cardboard cutout of a boy instead of the full-bodied, flesh-and-blood model.

"Why does he have it in for you?" Sam asked Matt as they headed to the basement for their biology lab. "What happened? Is this some ancient grudge?"

Matt shook his head. "No idea. Maybe because in our sixth grade Greek Games competition, I beat him in the 200-meter sprint, the hundred-meter sprint, the long jump and the final, most important, event of the day, the pie-eating contest." Matt grinned and pounded himself on the chest, swatting away Ella's hand as she tried to poke his stomach. "Reed is just a big coward who gets off on attacking anyone he thinks won't fight back. So Sam, the science competition has a lot at stake. It's us against them, good against evil, heaven against hell."

He grinned, rubbing his hands together, then paused, as if an uninvited thought had suddenly skidded across his mind: "And by the way, what awesome idea is going to win us first place?"

Chapter 2

Roof-top Visit

Sam ignored the tempting smells coming from Bella Vista's kitchen as the staff began prepping for the evening's four-star performance. "We need to start thinking about a topic. Now!" He looked at Matt, Ella, and Tristan gathered in the back corner of the empty dining room. "That's going to be more important than anything else we do for the next few weeks, right?"

Matt pumped his fist. "Right. Yeah, I'm psyched. And I'm hungry. Can we raid the kitchen for a quick snack? I think better when I'm full of protein."

"Protein?" Ella narrowed her eyes. She was sitting on a stool, her long, ash-blond hair caught up in a ponytail, her oversized sweater and collared shirt underneath covering the top of her jeans. "Why do I think it's not protein that you're after? And it's not really a kitchen that we're raiding. It's more like the bakery at a high-end department store, except that you don't have to pay for anything. But for you, Matt, I'm sure we can find some hard-boiled eggs."

Matt threw up his hands. "Okay, so I don't need to go heavy on the protein. But you have to admit: Brownies and cookies, or maybe a little cheesecake, a few cannoli sound perfect. You're so lucky, Sam, to be living in this place. Everything you want just one elevator ride away."

Everything I want? Sam repeated the phrase to himself. No. What I *want* is to go back to what my life was like a year ago. For that, I would trade all the desserts in the world. He took a deep breath: Keep looking ahead, moving forward, focusing on the present—phrases his father had spouted when they left their home and headed for a new beginning in a new city.

Matt was on the move. Incapable, as usual, of simply rising from a chair, he leapt up, landing squarely on both feet, hands raised, ready to sweep aside any and all enemies. It was a surprisingly nimble move for someone almost six feet tall who weighed close to 180 pounds and wore a size twelve shoe.

Sam followed him as he pushed through the swinging doors into the kitchen. "We're here!" Matt announced to the staff. "Is there any food that you're thinking of throwing away? We can help you with that."

Miguel, one of the younger members of the kitchen brigade and the only one with tattoos of angel wings on both his forearms, feigned a look of great relief. "Yes, we were wondering when the sanitation crew would come by. Without your help—especially yours, Matt—we would have been stuck with all the cleanup." He pointed to one of the countertops. "Here's a plate of food for your immediate *disposal*."

The cookies went first, then four pieces of cherry pie and finally, a wedge of blueberry cheesecake divided into four parts. Matt ate three of them. "I'm full," he announced. "I could use some fresh air." He widened his eyes at Sam, who gave his head the slightest nod. It was code for: roof time.

*****

On the 16th floor, at the end of a dark, musty storage area, Sam pulled down a trap door with steps going up to a small landing. He had found his way there just days after he and his father had moved into the hotel, when he was feeling caged in by the kitchen at one end, the new apartment at the other end, and a claustrophobic elevator connecting the two. Sneaking out onto the roof one afternoon, he had sensed for the first time that he could catch his breath, that there might be room for him here after all.

It was their third visit to the roof. Sam led the way as they climbed out through an unmarked steel door. And there it was, Manhattan on a dazzling January day—the windows of tall buildings catching the afternoon sun, cars like little Pac-Men slowly winding through the grid of avenues and streets, the southern border of Central Park opening up a world of trees and curving walkways that stretched as far as they could see.

"I bet no other kid in the school has anything like this," said Tristan. "It's big. It's quiet. No one knows where we are. We should make it our official science project meeting place."

Sam shook his head. "Listen, guys, I'm already feeling guilty about coming up here. We need to hold off, at least until I let my dad know what we're doing."

"In that case," said Matt, "I'm going to take one last look." He sprinted over to the low concrete parapet that ran along the roof and climbed onto it, taking a bow and then throwing up his arms against the wintry blue background of the sky.

Ella shrieked. "Matt! Get down, now! Do you hear me? Now! You're crazy! Sam, Tristan, tell him to get *off!*"

Sam ran up to Matt, stopping two feet from the ledge. "This is so *not* cool," he shouted at him. "If you don't get down in two seconds, I will never speak to you again." No response. "And I will never, ever let you into my kitchen for as long as I live."

Matt jumped down. "Okay, okay, relax. I wasn't in any danger. I wanted to see what it felt like to be that high. It was awesome, like I could lift off and fly anywhere I wanted, all the way up to that old monastery we visited or down to the Staten Island ferry. The whole world below me, and I would be on top. For once."

Ella looked at Sam and managed a quick smile. "Life without your father's cheesecake suddenly opened up before him," she whispered. "It's good to know what our *leverage* is."

Back in the fifteenth floor apartment, Sam collapsed on the living room couch. "Just in case I didn't make it clear, the roof is most definitely off limits, for now." He spoke to the group but finished up with a long, cold stare at Matt. "So let's move on. We need to start thinking about the science project. And remember, there's a lot riding on this. We could be the first science team our school sends to Washington, D.C., and the White House. We need an idea that is so creative, so unusual, that it will leave all the other teams eating our dust."

Chapter 3

When 'Best' Is the Worst

Sam walked out of Bella Vista's kitchen with a plate full of leftovers from the previous night's dinner and sat down next to his father. It was Monday, one week after the kickoff to the science competition. The dining room was closed to the public, which meant the two had the place to themselves.

"Our volleyball team won our second game on Friday, no thanks to me," Sam started off. "I stink. Our record is now two and five. You can safely skip the playoffs." He grinned: It was a joke. His father could never make it to any events that took place in the afternoon. It was one of the busiest times of the day for the pastry staff.

"But the big news is that ideas for the science projects have to be presented to a faculty committee for review in less than two weeks. If we're late, we automatically lose half a grade in the final scoring. Which means we need to come up with a big idea. Fast."

He paused again. Normally you would be all over this, Sam thought. But you're not. Something's wrong.

"Dad?" Sam felt a chill run up and down his back, the kind that usually signaled the arrival of very bad news. He stared at Nick, suddenly noticing how the chef's hat that always sat perfectly straight on his father's head was now tilted; actually it was drooping. And the pristine white chef's coat that always draped elegantly over his body, even on the crazy-busiest days, had food stains on the front and looked huge, like it had swallowed him up, leaving just his head poking out of the top.

"*Dad!*"

Nick's eyes finally focused on his son. "Sorry, Sam. I'm just thinking about the big event tomorrow night. Lots to do, and I'm behind on the design for the cake. It has to be really special." The thought hung for a moment in the air, more like a warning than a statement. "Really special. We'll talk later. You can tell me what's going on at school. I want to hear it all. But not right now. Too much to do."

He bent over so that his forehead rested briefly against Sam's own. It brought up the memory of many nights in their old house when Nick would come in late from work, tiptoe into Sam's room and gently tap his forehead against his son's. The lightest touch, but Sam always felt it, even in his sleep.

And then Nick was off. Sam stayed at the table. I'm right, he thought. Something's wrong.

****

Approximately twenty-four hours later, before the dinner guests were due to arrive at Bella Vista, Sam snuck into the back of the kitchen, his slender frame easily hidden by one of the big wooden cupboards. He knew that Simon, the head chef, always met with Nick before every dinner to confirm that final preparations for the dessert course had been completed. They had. Occupying the place of honor on a big round table off to the side was Nick's latest creation—a foot-tall chocolate cake in the shape of a Steinway grand piano, its tiny keys etched in with black and white frosting, the Steinway & Sons logo block-printed in sugar granules dyed gold.

"This is spectacular." Simon patted Nick on the back. "No

one in any of the five boroughs makes cakes this beautiful." He paused. His voice got softer, flatter. "Armand and Elaine just gave me the latest figures," he said, referring to the hotel's chief investor and property manager. "They're not good. Best and its splashy menu are killing us. It's like a big vacuum has suctioned up our customers and dropped them at Best's door two blocks away."

Simon and Nick walked towards the dining room, but Sam could still hear enough to get the message: A new restaurant called "Best" had opened in the same neighborhood and, within weeks, had become "the place to go." Bella Vista's dinner reservations were way down, which meant that the restaurant and its catering business were both losing money. Sam caught phrases like "shorter hours," "simpler menus," and then, more ominously, "possible layoffs" and "excellent references." He saw Nick's shoulders begin to sag, each pronouncement from Simon an invisible rolling pin pounding him lower and lower into the floor.

Sam caught his breath. He realized, in one of those hair-on-end thunderbolts of insight, that if Nick lost his job, they would have to move out of their home at The Meadows. Home? Had he really used that word? He had always described where he lived as "the staff apartment" or "the fifteenth floor." But it was home, even if his father didn't own it, even if there would never be room for a drum set. Apartment 15F was where he had been able to leave behind sad memories and to focus, as his father had advised, on the future.

Now, all of a sudden, his friends, his school, the big sprawling city he had only begun to explore—all seemed rootless, like the façade of a Hollywood movie set, two-dimensional, temporary. If an upstart new restaurant could destroy a foundation that had seemed so solid, then nothing was safe. Looking to the future didn't seem like such good advice after all.

Chapter 4

An Idea Is Born

Sam pulled Ella into a computer lab that had just emptied out. "Ella, I need to tell you something, but you have to promise not to tell anyone, okay?" He didn't wait for a response. "My dad's restaurant is in big trouble because a new place down the street is stealing a lot of its business. Bella Vista doesn't even have a waiting list for dinner reservations on the weekends anymore. I haven't seen him look this upset since..." He stopped.

"Why can't they just buy more advertising, or get someone to write a great review?" Ella quickly filled the silence. "My mother says it's the top restaurant in the city. She would know. She eats out with people from her company about every other night."

Sam shook his head. "It would take a lot more than one good review to turn things around. It's that whenever anything really hot comes up, people go chasing after it, like they're afraid it will disappear before they get to say they've been there. They don't care if a place closes and people are thrown out of work." Again.

Ella was looking at him strangely. "Come on. What are you thinking? You look like you've seen a ghost."

"No, no ghost." Just the memory of lives unraveled, turned upside down in the time it takes a shooting star to blaze across the sky and fall to earth. Best to improvise. "Yeah. So I just realized I don't have an article picked out for Harriton's class. With my luck, today is the day he'll call on me. I need something fast."

Ella headed down the hall. "Don't worry about your dad. Mine's always fretting about some crisis in the fashion business, and then it seems to get miraculously solved. Until the next one. Let's worry instead about the science project. Whatever we come up with, it has to be better than anything Reed and the super-obnoxious Charlene think of. I've decided I agree with Matt. This is about more than a science competition. It's about good versus evil, light versus dark, us against a bunch of bullying, blood-sucking lowlifes. Does that cover it?"

Sam burst out laughing, the shadows swept aside by Ella's alliterative rant. "Wow, Ell. I'm impressed. 'A bunch of bullying, blood-sucking lowlifes' pretty much says it all."

In a seat at the back of a nearly empty computer lab, he pulled up the latest edition of *The New York Times*. David Harriton, the notoriously demanding seventh grade history teacher, required his students to bring in a current events article every Wednesday and be prepared to summarize it for discussion. There were always muttered complaints about the relentlessness of the assignment— *every week?*—but Sam had to admit he always looked forward to this class more than any other.

His eye was caught by a weird headline on the *Times'* home page: "Colony Collapse Disorder: Cancel the Blueberry Pancakes." There was an even weirder photograph underneath showing a bunch of bees crawling over what looked like tiny empty cutouts in a cardboard milk carton.

The article described a syndrome that was causing the sudden disappearance of honeybees and the collapse of almost half the country's beehives. Since bees are responsible for pollinating most of the country's one hundred major crops—everything from apples, strawberries and blueberries to almonds, cucumbers and cantaloupes—Colony Collapse Disorder, or CCD, was having a devastating effect on big farmers and beekeepers. It could soon be felt by food shoppers as well: The article cited recent price hikes in the fruit and vegetable sections of local grocery stores.

In response to CCD, the *Times* article went on, more landowners were being encouraged to use fewer pesticides— including insecticides and herbicides (also known as weedkillers) —which some research scientists contend are toxic to bees in ways that aren't fully understood.

Sam focused on something else the article pointed out: Because of colony collapse, more and more people were becoming backyard beekeepers, setting up a few hives, or colonies, of their own in order to do their bit for the environment, but also to guarantee themselves a supply of honey. Some of them had joined a beekeepers association that advised city people on how to start their hives and—more importantly—where. Apparently it wasn't just backyards where hives could be found; it was also in community gardens, on apartment terraces, or wherever a tightly packed urban population could find space.

Including rooftops.

Bees, thought Sam. Beehives. Rooftops. An idea was stirring in the back of his head: honey … rooftops … bees … Bella Vista … science project. Was this the answer? He could hardly wait to get home.

*****

Sam cornered Nick in the kitchen just as the staff was cleaning up from the dinner service. "We did pretty well," Nick said, looking at the big piles of dirty dishes waiting to be washed. "Phew. I'm beat. Did you want to ask me something? You seem to be hovering." Nick smiled at his son.

He's in a good mood, Sam thought. So get the bad stuff out of the way now, like the fact that I hid in the kitchen so I could listen in on his private conversation with Simon.

He ran through it quickly, watching as Nick's face went from angry (red flush) to resignation (big sigh). "You're right, Sam," he said. "We're losing customers to Best. It's practically in our backyard, and its name is brilliant: Simple and easy-to-remember, and it suggests, with just one word, that its food is better than what you will find at any other restaurant."

Yes, Bella Vista was elegant, and the food was excellent, Nick said, "but Best is innovative and trendy. It's the new kid on the block. We're the old kid on the block. You're right about the waiting lists, too. They've just about evaporated."

In fact, Nick said, sometimes, at both lunch and dinner, there were empty seats. At Best, on the other hand, diners who hadn't been able to get reservations waited in the restaurant's lobby hoping to cash in on any last-minute cancellations. He gave a weak smile: "The joke going around is that unless a woman is having a baby *that moment*, or a man is having his gall bladder out *that night*, no one will give up a reservation. In short, Best is eating our lunch."

"What's worse," Nick continued, "is that Best's menu allows diners to choose a dinner by color." A red night might offer shrimp scampi, smoked beet casserole and cherries flambé. A green night might feature fettuccini verde, roasted asparagus and key lime pie. "It's gimmicky, but it's caught on. People aren't just talking about the meal. They compare dishes. They try to guess what Best's chefs will do next to create their color palettes...." He paused. "Armand

and Simon aren't optimistic. We're all wondering how long we can keep the place open."

That's my cue, Sam thought. The lines he had rehearsed earlier in the day came bubbling up. "So, Dad, what Bella Vista needs is its own way to stand out, something that isn't just a gimmick, something that people might think is clever but that also makes them feel good. When customers get tired of this color game—you said yourself they follow the latest trend—then you'll have something to bring them back to Bella Vista."

Nick rested a hand on Sam's shoulder. "I like that you have such faith in us. But tell me, just what exactly is that 'something?'"

"I'm working on it, Dad." Sam lifted his little finger to the corner of his mouth and raised his eyes to the ceiling—his best Mini-Me adaptation. It always got a laugh out of Nick. "I'll let you know when inspiration hits. For both of us."

Actually, inspiration had already hit. But before he could move ahead, there were three important people who needed to be shown the brilliance of his idea.

Chapter 5

Honeybee Liftoff

In the fenced-in basketball court behind the Manhattan School for Science, Ella, Matt, and Tristan were already huddled together trying to ignore the freezing drizzle. "You're late." Ella, her ponytail looped around and partially hidden under a big wool hat, shot Sam a hostile look as he walked up. The team had agreed to spend their lunch period outside where no one could overhear them brainstorming ideas for their science project.

"Sorry," Sam mumbled. "The Spanish quiz went long. But I'm here. Let's get started. We have a little more than a week to come up with an idea. Who's got one, even a half-baked one? Or should I say half-frozen one?" Okay, so he hadn't really expected anyone to laugh.

Ella pointed to Tristan. "You're the physics expert. We're counting on you for a dense, impenetrable, brilliant—"

"The impact force of falling objects," Tristan blurted out. "We could analyze different cushioning materials, like hard hats or rubber floors, to see how much they reduce the damage. Do you ever watch *MythBusters* on the Discovery channel? They had a show where they dropped a piano onto the roof of a house and tried to figure out its impact. We could do experiments, too. We could figure out which materials offer the most protection, depending on what's being dropped and what it's being dropped on. There's a lot of calculations involved. We'd have to do some work to learn them, but then we could build our own models, create some useful software programs. It's a project that would meet the 'relevance' criteria."

No one spoke. Tristan lightly rubbed a small scar—the result of a biking accident—that ran in a straight line across the bottom of his chin, its thin white ridges standing out in stark contrast to his brown skin. He does this, Ella had once told Sam, whenever he feels especially anxious or tense, like now, or when his brain is working overtime, a frequent occurrence. "Your enthusiasm is overwhelming," Tristan said. "Maybe I'll look into this sometime on my own. So who else has an idea?"

Ella piped up. "I was thinking about a project on how houses and office buildings could use more renewable energy. It would mean analyzing different alternative power sources, like solar, wind, and water and probably a bunch of others I don't know about."

She started to describe a trip with her parents to a home in southwestern Pennsylvania that was built over a waterfall. "It was designed by Frank Lloyd Wright, one of America's most famous architects, and it was the weirdest, most beautiful house I've ever seen, but what was really incredible was how—"

Matt interrupted her in mid-sentence: "But Ella, doesn't that just mean using solar energy for heating and cooling? Hasn't that already been done a lot? I mean what could we offer that's new? I'm not sure this makes for a whole project. Or at least, not a *winning* project."

Matt, as usual, was interested in winning, or, as he often put it: "It's not whether you win or lose. It's whether you win." Sam figured it came from having an older sister who happened to be a star—co-captain of the girls' soccer and tennis teams, captain of the debate team, a National Merit Scholarship finalist. Still, it couldn't hurt the project if Matt was driven by a need to be number one in something. I'm just as driven, Sam thought, and the consequences of losing are so much greater.

Ella glowered at Matt. "Okay, your turn. Make it fast. And it better be spectacular."

Matt glowered back. "Jeesh, Ella. Lighten up. Yeah, it's cold, but you don't have to turn into the wicked witch of the East ... or is it the West? I can never remember which witch is which ..." He began to laugh, but choked it off after a quick look at his audience. "Okay, so last night at dinner, we were kidding my mom about how every winter when we were little she would tell us to wash our hands whenever we touched anything outside the house—like a doorknob or a basketball or some other kid's backpack. We didn't do any of that and hey, we survived!"

Ella rolled her eyes. Matt sped up his delivery. "But maybe for our project we could look at different kinds of bacteria—why some grow, why some don't, which bacteria are the good guys and which are the really bad ones. My dad said we could test how heat and moisture and other things affect the spread of germs and why some people get really sick but others stay healthy. We'd have to get—"

It was Sam's turn to interrupt. "That sounds really good, Matt, except yesterday I heard Jamie talking to one of the science teachers about his team's idea to do what you just said—study 'microscopic organisms,' like bacteria and viruses and germs. They're planning to spend some afternoons working in a lab at Mt. Sinai Hospital where Jamie's mom happens to be head of the microbiology department. I would say they pretty much own that topic."

All eyes turned to Sam. "Okay, I have an idea, too. It's from reading *The New York Times* last week and then doing a lot of research. But before I tell you what it is, I'll tell you why it's good." He ignored the exaggerated calisthenics coming from Matt.

"We all know that Hineline is a tree hugger and an exercise freak," Sam said, referring to the teacher in charge of the seventh grade science curriculum. "For starters, she runs the New York Marathon every year, she has a community vegetable garden somewhere in Brooklyn, and she's always trying to organize hiking and kayaking trips." Which means, he went on, "she would probably be interested in a topic that has something to do with the environment... like honeybees."

Honeybees. The word floated up there, wafting lazily along in one of those comic book thought balloons. "So yeah, we could study what role bees play in our ecosystem, how they are one of our most important crop pollinators, how their hives are organized, but most importantly, why these days they're dying off by the millions. But I've saved the best for last."

He was speaking fast, trying to get it all out before the bell rang for fifth period. "We would set up our own hives on The Meadows' roof so we could learn about honeybees first hand. It means we could produce honey for ourselves and also give some to my dad for his restaurant. We would be the school's only rooftop beekeepers. We would be doing something relevant, meaningful, global ... all those syllabus words...." Sam paused.

Tristan reacted first. "I saw that same article in the *Times*," he said. "The hexagonal cells were amazing. The bees make them out of wax produced by their own bodies, and then use them to store honey.... It's almost like alchemy—creating complex systems out of very little material and in a very small space. Everything seems to work together so neatly, like some master plan was embedded in every bee's DNA. If we go ahead, I'll do the research on the structure of the hive."

Wow, thought Sam. Unlike me, he actually read the whole article and understood it, even the technical parts. No surprise there. He knew that Tristan's grandfather had been the only African American on the team of engineers responsible for designing one of the first personal computers. And no surprise either that Tristan had been accepted into a programming course offered two afternoons a week by Columbia University for exceptionally gifted middle and high school students.

"Tristan, you get it!" Sam offered a mock salute. "Not just the mechanics, but the mystery. I'm counting you as a 'yes.'"

That left two to go. Matt, staring off into space during Tristan's response, landed back on earth, a smile just beginning to light up his face. "So, despite what you said, we could go back on The Meadows' roof. Right? It could be our official meeting place, and we'd keep it stocked with our own private supply of high-nutrition baked goods—you know, to keep our brains functioning at the highest level." He smiled sweetly at Ella.

"So like you, Matt," she smiled sweetly back, "to focus on what's obviously the most important part of the project—your food intake. Or perhaps it's that we now have proof of what we always suspected, that your brains are in your stomach."

Even Matt had to laugh. "Yeah, I'm a walking medical miracle. But at least we won't be stuck in a lab all day, or even in the library. We would be doing research on living things...." He stopped. "But Sam, honeybees? Seriously? It sounds like the subject of a picture book for three-year-olds. I mean, is that topic complicated enough to win a prize?"

Tristan turned slowly around to face Matt. "Complicated enough? Matt, I don't think you get how complicated our environment is, and how bees play an incredibly important role in it, and how life in the hives is continually being studied because there is so much we still don't know about bee society."

He looked at Sam. "But I agree with Matt. We can't just recycle the same facts that people already know about bees. We need to come up with something else—like new data, or some experiment that no one has tried before. That's what would set our project apart. We wouldn't just be regurgitating what someone, somewhere, already knows."

Ella was next. Her response surprised everyone. "I can't imagine what I would do if honey disappeared," she said. "I put it on toast, pancakes, crackers, bananas, or I just eat it straight out of the jar. And it's in the Bible. You know, the land of milk and honey? That's what a lot of people lived on. Milk I could skip, but honey … So Sam, count me in."

The bell rang. "Honey on *bananas*?" Matt whispered to Tristan as the two of them headed off to class. Just before disappearing through the double doors, he turned back to Sam. "I know what we can call our project: 'No Bull, Just Buzz.'"

Sam could imagine a collective groan. He and Ella walked slowly back into the school building, a free period ahead of them before the next class. "I think we're on," he told her. "I think you tipped the balance."

Ella headed off for the library. "I meant what I said about honey. Just think of the hive—it's an efficient home, after all, and if you remember, that was the theme behind my idea for the project. A place where people, or insects, can live and work in ways that are resourceful and sustainable and communal—all those buzz words that people use when they talk about our planet."

Another smile and she was gone. Sam was reminded of his first day last September in a new school, one where most of the kids in his class already knew each other from the K-6 they had attended a mile away. He did the obligatory humiliating thing—fumbling through the lunch line and dropping his tray while he was looking for a seat, any seat, to slide in unnoticed. Suddenly a girl he had never seen before was there, tapping him lightly on the shoulder and motioning him to a nearby table.

"Here, sit with us," she said, leading him to a group of eight kids already midway through lunch. She pulled a chair over next to her seat. "What's your name?" she asked, then: "Hey, everybody, this is Sam." That's all it took. It was like landing on soft grass after being caught up in a windstorm. From that point on, the others simply absorbed him into their group—an ameba gently rolling along and pulling in an errant cell. Gradually, without any noticeable effort, he and Ella, Matt and Tristan became a subset within the set. A math class term that finally meant something real.

He never asked Ella why she had singled him out, and she never mentioned it. It was just like her. She didn't talk much about her parents or her two younger sisters. Sam knew that they lived in a townhouse on the Upper East Side, her father was an executive in a fashion company, and her mother was helping to launch a high-tech startup in one of the boroughs. And he knew, from Matt, that one of her sisters was diagnosed with bone cancer when she was eleven. The cancer was in remission, but the treatment had required amputation of her left leg above the knee.

And finally, he knew that Ella was often the one who cooked—or *assembled*, as she once described it—dinner when her parents worked late. Geez, Sam thought: She gets points as both a worker bee and the queen bee. Would she like that comparison? He wished he knew.

****

Sam sat on the kitchen stool at the end of one of the counters, aware that he had, at least for the moment, his father's full attention. "Okay, Dad, just sit down and don't say a word until I finish talking. I have one totally crazy idea that might help us both, but we'll have to get all sorts of permissions, and we'll need to clean up the roof a bit, and we'll have to get the right kind of hives and—"

Nick's voice jumped up an octave: "The *roof? Hives?* Sam, what are you talking about? Who's getting hives? On whose roof?"

In that brief moment, Sam realized he was about to experience a mind-bending, relationship-altering moment: He was going to lead his father down a path that could change their lives. "Listen, Dad, what if, as part of my science project, my team sets up some beehives on the roof of The Meadows, and we become beekeepers, rooftop beekeepers. It will be part of our report on this thing called 'Colony Collapse Disorder' which is destroying bee colonies and will probably make it harder to find the fruits and nuts you use in a lot of your pastries."

Sam went on to what he hoped would be the punchline. The rooftop hives, he said, would produce honey that Bella Vista could use, but that could also be given out to the restaurant's customers. "You would be sending a message to people about where their food comes from and why it's important to protect the environment. It won't be gimmicky, and it will make Bella Vista stand out like it used to."

Nick stared at his son. "So let's see if I get this. You and your team choose honeybees for your science project, and as part of your research, you become beekeepers on the roof of The Meadows?"

He paused for a minute, looking past Sam to a bin full of fresh vegetables. "Actually, our location is perfect, just a few blocks off Central Park. Hundreds of its trees and gardens rely primarily on bees for pollination."

Sam suddenly realized he wasn't sure how pollination actually worked. Oh, how that was going to change.

"At the right moment," Nick continued, "you and your team collect the honey, share it with Bella Vista, and it becomes a selling point for the restaurant." He paused. "Just how do you see that happening?"

Sam looked at the small containers of jams, jellies, and pâtés lining one of the long countertops. "Okay," Sam said. "What about if we—I guess that means you—create new dishes, even whole new menus, using the rooftop honey as one of the ingredients? And then you fill little pots with it and put them out on the dining room tables so that customers can take home whatever they don't use."

Nick began to pace around the counters. "With a clever design and colorful, new logo, it would be like an advertising campaign for the restaurant that happens to also support a good cause—the bees."

Sam bounced up and down on the stool. "Yes! And it wouldn't have to just be honey pots. We could also have honey lollipops, honey muffins, honey cookies, honey bubble gum…"

He stopped. Nick was smiling, laughing, the first joyous sound Sam had heard from him in weeks. I'm on a roll, he thought. Keep it going.

He explained how a lot of the action in the hives starts in the spring but gets really busy during June and July. He and his team would be around most of the summer to keep tending the bees. "I promise you that Bella Vista will get the first jar of home-grown honey, except that it will be roof-grown honey," he told Nick. No, he thought, "home-grown," if all goes as planned. "We could call it 'Honey from The Meadows.'"

He admitted the three rooftop visits, leaving off Matt's high wire act, and waited for his father to express disappointment, disgust, anger, or anything in between. But Nick barely seemed to have heard him. Instead, he took out an order pad and began to make notes. "The first thing to do is present this idea to my bosses. You'll be the main speaker, so I suggest you do some homework and come up with solid information," he said.

"Me?" Sam knew his voice had just squeaked. "Present to your bosses? Why not you? I mean, you know them. You know the restaurant and everything needed to make this happen. We haven't even done much research yet...."

Nick cut him off with a smile. "Well then, you've got a lot of work ahead of you."

Chapter 6

2,000 Eggs a Day

The countdown was beginning. In seventy-two hours, a group of eight faculty members would decide which ideas were good enough to sustain a semester-long project.

"How do we convince them?" Sam addressed the team as they sat in a glassed-in study room at the back of the school library. "To start, we have to make honeybees so totally interesting and important that everybody wants to know a lot more about them. Which means *we* need to know a lot more about them. So," he said, turning to his laptop. "Allow me to present you with highlights from my three hours of research, beginning with a video showing you a hive arriving in the mail to a beekeeper in Queens."

The opening scene showed hundreds of bees moving quietly, almost meekly, out of a container the size of a shoebox into a wooden hive set in the middle of a small garden filled with wildflowers. The beekeeper, according to the voiceover, had lost his hives to a plague of varroa mites and was trying to start a healthy new colony.

"What got me," Sam said, "is the way each bee knows exactly what she has to do, like she's following the orders of some invisible drill sergeant. And by the way, I do mean 'she,' but more on that later. Look, the bees are just making an orderly exit—no pushing or shoving, no butting in—even though their ride through the U.S. postal service must have been incredibly uncomfortable."

And then they get inside the hive, and each one, according to the narrator, immediately goes to work setting up her new home. "How do they know what their duties are, and why aren't they bumping into each other or fighting over who gets the bigger space or the easier job?" Sam asked. "And what are those jobs? What are they doing in there?"

He quickly threw out some more facts. The hive is ruled by females, including the queen bee, who gets fed a special high-protein food that makes her bigger than all the others. "And that's a good thing," Sam went on, "because she has a lot of work ahead of her—like laying 2,000 eggs a day—about a million in total over her lifetime. They hatch mostly into female worker bees, but there are also a few males, called drones, whose main job is to mate with a new queen. Once they do that, they die."

Matt broke in: "What a waste. All that manpower cut off in the prime of its life. I think bee culture needs a do-over, starting with a king bee at the top."

"Sure thing, Matt," said Ella. "Then it's the king who can be surrounded by all the workers, smothered or stung to death and tossed out of the hive. That's what happens to the queen after she can no longer lay eggs. Right, Sam? I've been doing some research, too."

Sam nodded. "Yeah, unfortunately the queen's last days don't always go well for her…. But moving on, if something bad happened to bees, we would lose about one-third, maybe more, of our entire food supply. What does that mean, you might ask," he said. No one did. "And even more important, which third of our food supply are we talking about?" Again, blank faces.

I'm losing my audience, Sam thought. Time for inspiration. He grabbed his backpack. "Come on," he said. "We're going food shopping."

A short subway ride, and they were a block away from a big grocery store near The Meadows. Sam led the way into the fruit and vegetable section. "Watch me," he said, taking off down the aisle. He stopped every few steps and pointed to bins of strawberries, apples, apricots, blueberries, cantaloupes, peaches and grapes. He moved down another aisle filled with asparagus, celery, cucumbers, zucchini, squash, and all kinds of beans.

"Are you getting the picture?" he asked. "If bees are no longer around to pollinate these crops, they'll be in much shorter supply, and they'll probably cost a lot more. Next, the nuts." He pointed to bags of almonds and cashews.

Matt's jaw dropped open. "Almonds? What about Almond Joys and Snickers and Cashew Butter Crunch and all that?" He grabbed his throat and gasped for air.

"Yep," said Sam. "You might have to start looking for substitutes. That also goes for jams and jellies."

Honey made its appearance on the next shelf. Clover and orange blossom looked like big sellers. "Honey's taste and color depends on what flowering plants the bees are getting their nectar from," Sam said. "What's amazing is that a single bee produces only 1/12th teaspoon of honey in her lifetime. So each of these jars represents a huge team effort."

He moved on to the display case of the bakery section and tapped the glass in front of coconut bars, chestnut pralines, muffins, strawberry shortcake, and cherry, apple, and peach pies. "Oh, and forget pumpkins at Halloween and watermelons. Bees pollinate those, too."

Tristan approached a small kiosk near the cash registers that sold bouquets of flowers, gift-wrapped assortments of spices, beeswax candles, and other items for the last-minute shopper. "Better add these to the list."

Ella sighed. "I guess that includes wildflowers—all those beautiful plants you see in the gardens around Central Park. If these tiny pollinators ever become an endangered species, it could shut down our whole planet. Would people—*us?*—start disappearing from grocery store aisles along with everything else? It would make a great plot for a sci-fi movie."

Chapter 7

Fire Drill Rescue

The loud beep-beep-beep caught everyone at the Manhattan School for Science by surprise. Sam joined packs of reluctant students shuffling outdoors at the slowest possible speed to stand in the frigid air while the fire safety committee went through its compliance check.

Milling around with a group of seventh graders, he realized after a few moments that Tristan was nowhere to be seen. I know what's going on, Sam thought. Tristan's in a computer lab, and his concentration is so intense that he probably didn't hear the alarm, didn't notice that all the other kids were filing out of the room, and he was the only one left.

Sure enough, a teacher, shaking her head, soon appeared at the school door with her hand on Tristan's back propelling him not-so-gently forward. As he moved into the crowd, Reed and Miles came up on either side and began a barrage of taunts. "What's the matter, Tristan? Are you deaf?" Reed hissed in his ear. "Or just dumb?"

No-neck Miles, looking like R2-D2 in a down jacket, had the other ear: "Or maybe you just don't like people. Come to think of it, I'm not sure I've ever seen you actually talk to a live human being, just those machines. Do they talk back?"

Seconds before Tristan was completely surrounded, Ella was there, pretending to trip and fall against the back of Reed's knee, hard enough that he lost his balance and finally fell, arms flailing, into a puddle on the ground. "So sorry," Ella said, glancing down at him. "I wasn't looking where I was going. I would offer to help you, but I don't want to get my hands dirty."

Sam caught up with Tristan once the all-clear signal sounded. "So, are you really excited about our project, or were you hoping for a more scientific, tech-oriented idea?" he asked. "Sometimes I can't really tell."

Tristan hadn't spoken much since his comments about the hive. But then he rarely said much on any occasion, even in class. He's not shy, someone had once told Sam; he's *thinking*. Which made sense, Sam thought. Tristan was so much more comfortable in front of a screen than in front of people,

"No, I'm good," Tristan said. "Bees are pretty exciting—orderly and efficient, and then there's all those chemical reactions that go on in the process of making wax and honey and everything else. Humans could probably learn a lot from observing their social structure. But let's be careful not to anthropomorphize them. It would take away from the seriousness of our research."

"Sure," Sam said, peeling off for the library. "Whatever that means, we won't do it. I promise."

Chapter 8

Enemy Attack

Sam stared at the charts and illustrations the team had created for its faculty presentation. Each had been torn into pieces and smeared with what looked like honey and jam packets from the cafeteria. Even the easel had been attacked, its spindly frame smashed into what looked like a collection of broken bones. "I think the science competition has just been ratcheted up to a new level," he said, his voice shaking. "Any doubt who did this? We should have hidden our stuff in a locked closet instead of leaving it in the storage area."

Matt began to collect some of the pieces while Tristan leaned silently against the wall, trying not to look at the wreckage. It doesn't fit in with his image of a rational, orderly world, thought Sam.

Ella knelt for a closer inspection. "Leave it to the Evil Ones to choose honey as their weapon," she said. "But the big question is, how do we fix this in the next twenty-four hours? Our presentation to the faculty is tomorrow at two." No one answered.

"Wait a minute!" Ella jumped up. "Maybe we *don't* fix this. Maybe we let the broken pieces tell the story of Colony Collapse Disorder. You know, like we intended all along to present an image of destruction, of things falling apart, of how life on this planet would become degraded, *splintered*, without bees and pollination. We just have to figure out how to use all this mess to our advantage."

She presented a step-by-step strategy. Start by skipping last period—"desperate times call for desperate measures." Put all the broken pieces in whatever bags they could find. Take the subway to The Meadows. Stop in the kitchen for "protein to power us through the night." Head up to Sam's living room. "Then we'll assemble the presentation we would have made—without the scorched-earth attack—and reorient it to dramatize our message about bees and CCD."

Matt looked at Ella. "There's one part of the plan that you left out. Revenge. They're not getting away with this. After tomorrow, we decide what to do, when to do it, and how to do it for maximum impact. This is stealth warfare. We're dedicated warriors, fighters for the good, avengers of stolen honor..."

I wonder what video game he's been playing now, Sam thought as they headed out to the street. "Good idea, Ell, although I have no idea how we'll pull it off. I mean Reed made sure we have almost no time to fix this. He thinks of everything. And he never seems to get caught."

******

"I feel like we're in line for the guillotine," Ella mumbled the next morning as they sat in the hallway with the other three teams assigned that day to present their science competition ideas to a faculty panel. "Off with their heads!" She tried to giggle but it sounded more like a strangled hiccup.

We're all jittery from exhaustion, Sam thought, trying to calm himself by estimating the combined number of hours the team had slept last night. About twelve, he decided, watching Matt shift his weight from side to side while Tristan barely moved, the palm of his hand massaging the scar on his chin in tight little circles.

Down the hallway, Reed's team, now officially known as "Robots R Us," banged restlessly against the walls like a pack of caged, hungry wolves. The auditorium door opened, and a faculty member beckoned them in. Exactly fifteen minutes later, they came out, Reed's long neck swiveling from side to side as though acknowledging accolades from a crowd of admirers. The team high fived each other and swaggered down the hall, too cocky to bother taunting the remaining presenters.

The door opened again, and a teacher called out the names of the bee project team, then pointed to a table and chairs lined up in place of the front row. "You have fifteen minutes to convince the faculty of the merit of your proposal," she announced, sounding more robot than human. "Go."

Ella went first. She quickly set up the easel, patched together and covered with pieces of a torn menu. The panel could just barely make out a selection of appetizers, entrees, and desserts, none of which included vegetables or fruits. "Our project looks at the dangers facing the honeybee population due to a convergence of events that scientists are calling 'Colony Collapse Disorder', or 'CCD,'" Ella stated, as Matt put out a few small bowls of cherries and almonds. She briefly explained different theories about the causes of CCD, and noted that the team would explore them in depth in their report.

She passed around charts and graphs, some of them with slash marks and ripped edges to drive home the consequences of CCD devastation. On cue, Matt snatched away the fruit and nuts just as three of the teachers reached for them.

Tristan and Matt were up next: They unveiled the second poster—a chart, hastily reconstructed the night before, outlining the steps by which honey is produced, including pollination. On the third poster, a large drawing of the inside of a hive was defaced by magic marker scribbles. Globs of discolored, sticky honey and jam remained smeared around the edges, suggesting once again, Tristan said, the havoc that CCD has inflicted on bees and the environment.

And finally, Sam. He explained their plan to set up beehives on top of a landmark Manhattan hotel, and then ended by showing a photograph of The Meadows' roof, photoshopped to include bees and beehives. The fifteen-minute buzzer sounded.

Sam managed a quick look at the faculty as the team gathered up their materials. Most of them seemed, if not impressed, at least not skeptical. Only one—Suzanne Bowers, a tenth grade biology teacher—raised her hand to speak to the panel. "Given that we don't allow time for questions, I will just say that I feel this project idea is gimmicky and unoriginal, with nothing to suggest that it will go beyond your typical middle school science report on a much studied insect population."

An awkward silence followed. Sam heard Stephen Cain, the school's science resources coordinator, respond just before the door was shut. "I understand what Suzanne is saying, but I would add that the students have made a good case for the importance of studying honeybees at this pivotal point in time, when so many of them are dying off for as yet unexplained reasons. Provided this project offers serious, in-depth analysis, I would suggest we accept the proposal."

Chapter 9

Snakes & Screams

The next morning, a short email from the head of the science department went out to the four teams that had appeared before the faculty panel the day before. All four ideas had been accepted.

"I think the almonds and cherries, or rather their sudden disappearance, did it," Sam said to Ella as he set out his carton of orange juice and a cranberry nut muffin brought from home. "In any case, we made it!" he added, all his energy focused on trying to pry open the carton without spilling the juice.

Ella, slumped in a chair next to him in the school's cafeteria, didn't respond. Sam looked up in time to see her angrily brush away a sudden rush of tears. "Ell! Are you crying? What's going on? What's wrong?"

She slapped a single sheet of paper onto the table. It was a crude drawing of a young girl with only one leg being attacked by a bunch of winged insects. Underneath was the caption: "One-legged wonder can't outrun horde of killer bees." Ella wiped her eyes. "It was pasted to the door of my locker. I can't believe someone would be this evil. Except, of course, that I know who it was."

She sank even lower in the chair. "In case you hadn't guessed, it's supposed to be my sister. It's not like her leg is a secret. At our sixth grade graduation, everyone watched Allison walk up and give me a bear hug as I came off the stage. Kids know that nothing stops her: She can throw a fastball faster than anyone on the softball team and shoot ten baskets in a row. She's one of the most popular girls in her class."

Ella closed her eyes for a moment, then tore the paper into little bits and tossed them into the big trash can by the door, just as Tristan and Matt walked in. "Hey, guys, what's up?" Matt asked, his eyes devouring Sam's uneaten muffin. Tristan glanced quickly at Ella and sat down, silent.

At least she's stopped crying, Sam thought, listening to Ella's brief explanation. Matt pounded his fist on the table so hard that an arc of orange juice spurted out onto the muffin. "Is there any doubt who did this?"

Ella shook her head. "No. It's Charlene. I saw her staring at me during first period to see if I was upset, so I tried to act normal, like nothing was wrong. What are we going to do? We can't pretend this didn't happen."

Sam looked at Tristan. I'm not giving him a pass on this, he thought. He can't just clam up as if it doesn't affect him. "Tristan! You haven't said a word. Do you agree we have to do something? Any ideas? *Anything?*"

Tristan flinched. "Okay, guys. Yeah, so I'm not good at picking up signals." He hesitated. "But I get it. I know how Ella feels. I know that we need to respond in a way that reflects the seriousness of the situation."

Matt grinned: "What you mean is, 'Time for Immediate Revenge.' And I happen to have a plan."

Charlene, everyone knew, was totally, deathly, obsessively afraid of snakes. Two years ago, during a fifth grade class trip to the Museum of Natural History, the guide assigned to them had paused for a teaching moment in front of cages full of reptiles. Charlene was whispering nonstop to a friend during the presentation and hadn't seen the guide pull a six-foot long yellow gopher snake out of the cage and swing it gently in an arc in front of his visitors. When Charlene turned her head to see what her friend was looking at so intently, she was staring at her worst nightmare ten feet away.

The shriek reverberated off the walls and along the corridors of the museum's fourth floor, Ella said. It was as though someone stuck Charlene's whole body into an electrical outlet and turned up the power. Five museum guards rushed in ready to arrest some troublemaker and instead, walked off shaking their heads and chuckling. "It's probably the only thing any of us remember about that day."

Snakes? No problem. Sam led the way to a science lab that had just been opened by one of the school administrators. Among spiders, moths, dragonflies, and toads was a cage full of harmless gray garter snakes munching on earthworms and snails.

"Too bad Charlene isn't afraid of something more interesting, like pigeons or vampire bats," Matt said.

"Vampire bats? In New York City?" Sam asked, forgetting for a moment how pointless it was to ever engage in Matt-logic. "Never mind, just hurry up. We have to get out of here, fast."

Matt reached in, pulled out the biggest snake, and put it in a paper bag that had, ten minutes ago, contained his day's worth of snacks. "For good luck, I'm adding some spiders and worms," he said, handing the bag to Ella.

She paused. "Just so you know, this means Charlene and company are probably going to strike back in some totally disgusting way. It's okay for you guys, but I have to see her every day in the locker room. I'll be the target, not you."

It was Tristan who responded. "The question to ask ourselves," he said quietly, "is what should we, or anyone, do when mean kids decide to make us a target? As it is, we don't retaliate because we're afraid it will only make things worse and because we're worried that none of the other kids will support us. But what if we *did* hit back? Then bullies might start to worry about *us*. They're not used to being on the other side of the line. We never think how *they* would react if *they* were the victims, if all of a sudden *they* had to look over their shoulders."

By now, his voice had dropped almost to a whisper. "Think about it: Aren't there usually more kids who are bullied than there are bullies?"

Tristan talking about *retaliation?* The team was definitely bonding, Sam thought, wondering just how many times over the years Tristan had been picked on by kids bigger, meaner, and dumber.

Ella reached for the paper bag. "Tristan's right. I know it's not exactly what the books say, but I don't care. Charlene deserves everything we're giving her. Why should we be the ones to back off and not her?"

Outside the lab, the team split up—Sam and Tristan to Spanish class, Matt to English, Ella to the girls' locker room.

When the bell sounded for the end of second period, the team headed to the lockers to change out their class materials for the rest of the morning. Within two minutes, the basement's calm undercurrent of chatter was broken by what Tristan later said was the *loudest* screech he had ever heard. Sam would say it was the *longest* screech he had ever heard. For Matt, the most *satisfying* screech. Ella never mentioned it, that day or any other. She came out of the locker room, hoisted her backpack, and walked silently down the hall. Message delivered. Time to move on.

Chapter 10

Birth of The Bee Team

Science Project Idea Agreed on by Team: Check

Science Project Idea Proposed to Faculty Committee: Check

Science Project Idea Accepted by Faculty Committee: Check

Science Project Research Started:

"So how are we going to organize the research for our project, or rather *who's* going to organize it?" Sam looked at Tristan, who looked at Ella, who looked at Matt, all of them perched on top of Bella Vista's kitchen worktables. "We're already way behind. Some of the other teams are meeting almost every day in the cafeteria. I see them hunched over their laptops, taking notes, looking at books, collaborating. We need to start moving."

Three sets of eyes turned to Sam. "So move," said Matt. "It was your idea in the first place."

Sam had prepared for this moment. "Okay. First off, we need to get permission from the city to set up the hives. Second, we need to figure out how to order the bees. Third, we need to study bee colonies, pollination, life in the hive, how honey is made, and get the latest information about colony collapse since that's what everyone is talking about, or at least everyone in the bee world. Plus it makes our project that all important word—'relevant.'"

He gave out assignments. Ella would look into colony collapse, Matt into pollination and honey production, and Tristan into bee life and bee society. Sam would research how to order the bees and bee equipment, plus check out space on the roof, and last of all, come up with a cost estimate.

"Hey, you have the best job!" said Matt. "The roof part, I mean. Can't we all go up and check out the space?"

"Sure, we can all do that," Sam said, deciding that Matt did not share the worker bee trait of doing the job he was assigned without complaining. "And let's report back to each other on Thursday. Our first team deadline. One more thing. We need a name for ourselves."

Matt jumped up, scattering cookie crumbs on the floor. "I've got it. How about 'The Honey Bunch?'" Ella pretended to put her finger down her throat. "That bad?" Matt mouthed the words.

"That bad," she mouthed back. "Besides, I have a better idea. What if we call ourselves 'The Bee Team'? It's short, direct, it's obviously a pun, and it immediately gets people to ask, 'Why aren't they calling themselves 'The A Team?'"

Tristan's response, concise and to-the-point as usual, sealed the deal. "I like it. It combines the two most important parts of our project—the bees and us, the team."

Sam made it official: "From this moment on, apiarists— that's what they call beekeepers—we will forever be known as the Manhattan School for Science's unbeatable Bee Team."

****

An hour later, Matt's self-appointed role as de facto poison tester for the Bella Vista kitchen was winding down for the day. He snatched the last chocolate-dipped macaroon from a dessert platter just as Nick walked in to begin decorating a large rectangular cake in the shape of the Madison Square Garden ice hockey rink, its smooth surface dotted with small, plastic New York Rangers pro hockey players, two goalie cages made of peanut brittle, and a tiny chocolate puck.

"Only one, Matt?" Nick asked, raising his eyebrows in mock horror. "Please, take the whole plate. And there are more of them in the fridge. Our poison tester needs to stay on top of his game."

Matt, Sam was surprised to see, actually turned red, then pretended to gag on the macaroon. "I'd say this one has a *touch* of arsenic, or perhaps a *dash* of hemlock. Maybe Bella Vista needs some new chefs?" He closed up his backpack and waved goodbye to Nick and the others. "Off to get my stomach pumped. Thanks for the snacks."

"Food brings out the best in Matt," Ella grinned, then gave Tristan a gentle shove. "We're out of here, too. See you tomorrow."

"Dad," Sam said as the door shut. "I'm feeling good. I think we're all getting what it is about bees that's so amazing. Their teamwork, the way they do everything for the good of the hive. There's no infighting, no inflated egos, no slacking off. And they pollinate fruits, vegetables, trees, flowers more efficiently than any system we could possibly make up."

"Yeah, and look at us," Nick said, shaking his head. "We've managed to create a society that's in danger of killing them off. Bees have been around for what, millions of years? And here our highly sophisticated, technologically advanced, space age civilization seems to be doing nothing as they're all destroyed."

Sam let out a whoop. "Wow, Dad, nice going! You've just written the final sentence in our report. Consider yourself an honorary team member. From now on, you're responsible for all our brainy-sounding conclusions plus our afternoon snacks."

Nick smiled. "I think I've been responsible for that second item from the moment your friends set foot in this kitchen."

Sam felt his stomach do a sudden flip. Time for an update. "Dad," he said. "I don't suppose anything has changed about the restaurant? I mean, are things still not looking good? And what about us? Your job, our apartment, my school?"

Sam thought of those carnival masks that have a sunny, smiling face on one side, and on the other, a dark frown, eyebrows drawn together into a scowling "V." Nick's face was "the other."

"No, Sam, nothing's changed." Nick's voice was subdued. "The hotel has told me that it won't take any action for a few months, maybe even until the beginning of the fall when people return from their summer vacations. But they also told me to make sure my resumé is together and ready to send out." The fact is, he added, pastry chefs are not exactly a hot property. "Head chefs, yes. Good ones are always in demand because a restaurant's reputation can rise and fall on their success."

Sam knew that Nick had a reputation, too—a chef whose name had appeared in local newspaper and magazine articles as the creator of amazing pastries and cakes in the shape of an Amtrak train, a Big Mac, a 747 jetliner, a fairy princess, a roller skate, a violin. But Sam also knew it probably wasn't enough to get a job anything like the one Nick had now, in a top-flight restaurant in a landmark hotel with a two-bedroom apartment that looked out on the vast expanse of Central Park.

"So, what does that mean for us?" Sam asked, hating the

tremble in his voice. "Will we have to leave New York?"

Nick came over to Sam and gave him a quick hug. "I honestly don't know," he said. "But if you can convince Armand and Elaine and Simon that honey from The Meadows' hives can help revive Bella Vista—well, it can't hurt."

He looked at his watch. "I have to get the icings going, and you have to do your homework. Let me know when you might be able to make your pitch to the bosses. And if you feel nervous, think of it this way: What do you have to lose?"

Sam repeated the phrase to himself as he got on the elevator. What do I have to lose? Let's see: How about the science competition, a four-star food source, a home at the top of a luxury hotel, a city I belong in … and Ella.

Chapter 11

Sam Makes the Case

"This is the way I felt last summer when I interviewed for the scholarship at school," Sam whispered to Nick, "except this is worse. What if they don't like the idea? What if they ask me questions I can't answer? What if they just don't like me?"

Sam and Nick were sitting on a bench outside Armand's office on the second floor of The Meadows. The hotel's chief investor, along with its property manager and Bella Vista's head chef, had agreed to meet with them for ten minutes on a busy Wednesday afternoon.

Nick sounded exasperated. "Sam, we have rehearsed your speech at least five times. And of course they like you. You already know Simon and Elaine, and I introduced you to Armand when we first moved in. As far as I can remember, no one held their nose when they met you. So chill. Just be your normal, friendly self. The worst they can do is turn down your idea."

Total disaster, Sam thought. "Then what happens?" he asked Nick. "We don't have much time to come up with anything else. Every other team is way ahead in their research—"

He was interrupted by Armand's assistant. "Armand is ready for you," he said. "And please keep the meeting to the scheduled ten minutes. He has another appointment right after this one."

Sam felt Nick's hand guide him over to a couch surrounded by chairs and a coffee table. The three executives were already there, looking as if they were expecting to be served a slightly unappetizing meal and were trying to think how they could politely put it down the disposal. "Sam," said Armand brusquely, pulling the vest of his three-piece suit over a stomach that appeared to have digested more than its share of Bella Vista's pastries. "You're on. Tell us what you want."

"Yes, sir," said Sam. "I am a student at the Manhattan School for Science. We—my science team; there are four of us—want to do our science project on honeybees. We'll be studying the life cycle of bees and how they make honey, and we'll also be studying colony collapse and what that means for our environment. Everyone says it could be—"

Armand interrupted, as Nick had warned he liked to do. "Yes, yes, I know about honeybees and honey. And you can explain colony collapse some other time. What does all this have to do with me?" he asked, looking at his watch.

Get to the point, Sam told himself. "Yes, sir. As part of our study of bees, my team would like to set up four honeybee hives on The Meadows' roof. We would order them this spring, assemble them, get the bees, and then in July and August, we would use the honey we collect as part of our project. But more importantly, we would give most of it to Bella Vista. Simon and my dad and the other chefs could use it in new recipes, and you could design a logo and put it on little containers of honey that customers take home with them. It would be a way to bring more attention to the restaurant, to get people talking about Bella Vista again … and it would be seen as cool to know that you're helping the environment.…" He was beginning to wind down, but at least Armand wasn't looking at his watch.

Now it was Simon's turn to break in. "Do we have any idea how hard it is to set up hives and take care of them?" he asked, leaning forward so that his hands—surprisingly round and white, like big, doughy dumplings—rested on his knees. "Who's going to pay for all this? Bees cost money. Hives cost money. I'm sure the equipment costs a *lot* of money."

Armand again: "Letting people up on our roof would require a number of safety checks, but I seem to remember that at one time, we actually held receptions up there. I'm not sure how much work that took, or whether those events made any money...."

And finally, Elaine, the property manager, her black stiletto heels almost as lethal as the carving knives in Bella Vista's kitchen: "Don't we need to do a lot of research before even one hive gets set up? Research, dependable research, is always more expensive than you expect."

"Elaine," said Nick. "The money isn't a problem." He pointed to his son. "Sam and his team are totally committed to this idea, and in fact they have spent the last few weeks looking into the permit issue and collecting information about bees and hive care and pollination and all that. You have excellent researchers already on board, and you won't have to pay them a dime."

But it shouldn't just be about money, Sam thought. "One more thing. What I'm really hoping is that this project helps a lot of people understand how extraordinary bees and pollination are, and how their hives, their social structure, their teamwork... how all these things are so important to our planet. If we lose our bee population, it would be a catastrophe." He stopped, sensing that Armand was no longer listening.

And the verdict? This is a group that makes decisions quickly, Nick had said. You will probably have your answer before you leave the room.

He didn't. Armand looked at his colleagues: "It's an interesting idea, but I don't have enough information to know if it's worth the trouble for us to be involved. Agreed?" Simon and Elaine nodded.

"Sam," Armand went on. "Check into the permission angle, and figure out how much honey we would get from your hives. Are there any downsides for us in agreeing to your proposal? Analyze what could go wrong. Most importantly, where do you think you will get the money to finance all this? As Simon pointed out, you're talking about hundreds of dollars, probably thousands. I need some idea of how you plan to pay for everything so that The Meadows doesn't find itself with a bunch of empty hives cluttering our roof."

The meeting was over. "Give me a memo with the answers to these questions, and I'll get back to you." And if the project moves forward, he added, "we would need to get a roofer up there for a safety check. The liability issues could be another problem, perhaps an insurmountable one."

On the way to his office he paused for a moment and looked back at Sam: "I have to say, honey has always been one of my best memories from childhood. My mother used to put it on little pieces of banana and stick them into my Hopalong Cassidy lunchbox. I ate them for snack every day. What a mess. And how wonderful they tasted."

Chapter 12

Doing the Waggle Dance

"Where the heck is this place? Outer Mongolia?" Matt, followed by his teammates, trudged down unfamiliar hallways in the school's basement.

"Maybe we should leave a trail of little pebbles," Tristan suggested. "You know, like Hansel and Gretel, so we don't get lost coming back."

"Hey, guys." Sam knew he sounded impatient. "What are we going to say to Carlisle?"—a reference to their mandatory meeting with Helen Carlisle, the teacher assigned to advise them on the science competition. "We're supposed to have some kind of progress report completed. And we don't, at least not a formal one. Let's hope the research we've done is enough."

Matt blew past Sam's comment: "I've got a question: Why did we get Carlisle as our advisor? It was probably Bowers' idea—another way to sabotage us. Carlisle's been around forever, and all she does down here is tutor the kids who are flunking biology."

Ms. Carlisle loomed in the doorway, her large, pear-shaped body blocking the light behind her, and summoned them into a classroom that looked like it had been swept up in a tornado and never fully reassembled. Sam walked carefully around a display of partially decomposed insect skeletons.

"Welcome, Tristan, Ella, Sam, and Matthew." Ms. Carlisle, wrapped in a faded, gray cardigan that probably dated back to the musty, decaying experiments scattered around her, settled into the chair behind her desk.

"I have read your science proposal, and I must say, it is certainly ambitious." Her attempt at a smile flat-lined. "Getting bees on the roof of a hotel will be no easy task, but I trust you will have the necessary permissions to make this happen. So we will not spend time today going into that. Instead, tell me some of the interesting things your research has unearthed so far. Tristan?"

Tristan pulled from his backpack several photographs of a hairy, globular-shaped, bug-eyed little creature with three pairs of legs, nearly transparent wings, crooked antennae and other strangely shaped appendages. "What's amazing," he said, "is that every part of a bee's body serves some purpose."

Exhibit One: The proboscis, a long pointy tongue at one end of the bee's head. "It's like a straw to help field bees suck out nectar from the flowers. They carry it back to the hives and transfer it to house bees. The house bees fan it with their wings until eighty percent of the moisture in the nectar evaporates. What's left begins to thicken and turn into honey."

Exhibit two: Tiny baskets on the hind legs of forager bees. "They're like the saddle bags on a bike, except they're used to store pollen that rubs off on a bee while she's extracting the nectar." He pointed to what looked like thick, yellow earmuffs attached to each leg. "Back in the hive, the pollen gets mixed in with enzymes from a bee's own body, and, presto, it becomes 'bee bread,' the hive's main source of protein."

Exhibit three: Wings. "The membranes are so thin you can actually see through them," Tristan said. "A honeybee flaps her wings about 250 times a second. When she can no longer fly, her sisters kick her out of the hive. Bees also use their wings to keep the queen cool while she produces all those eggs."

Exhibit four: Eyes. "Bees have five of them," he noted, pointing out two large ovals and three smaller circles on his diagram. "Scientists think that bees don't see the color red—only yellow, blue-green, blue, orange, and violet. They also see ultraviolet, which is invisible to us, but helps bees determine which flowers have nectar."

And finally, the stinger. Tristan indicated a sharp pointed object at the end of the bee's body—"a sac that stores venom. But honeybees don't sting as an act of aggression, like wasps or yellow jackets. Bees sting only if they feel their hive is being threatened, if they get stepped on, or if their flight path is seriously interrupted." In most cases, he added, a bee's insides are ripped out during the act of stinging, and she dies.

Tristan pulled out his last note card. "But what's possibly the most amazing thing about bees is the weird little 'waggle dance' they do when they return from their foraging trips. By performing a series of figure-eight moves at various angles and speeds, a bee tells the other bees where to find nectar—how far away and in what direction. It's radar for a colony of aviators ¾ of an inch long."

As if responding to some invisible cue, Matt began to move ever so slightly back and forth, his shoulders rising, his chin jutting out, and then it was maximum liftoff—a rocket shot out of the chair, arms outstretched, body in full sway. "Like this," he said, swinging his hips from side to side and his head up and down while his hands carved out a circle and his fingers pointed in four different directions.

"North, South, East, West," he chanted before spinning around the room a few times and finally sitting down.

Ms. Carlisle looked at Matt. "That was enlightening, Matthew," she said, her lips barely moving. "If you're not too exhausted, why don't you give us your report." It didn't sound like a question.

"My subject is pollination," Matt said, quickly pulling out a few loose papers from his backpack, "and it goes like this: A bee lands on the male part of a flower, called the anther, and sucks up the nectar. While that's going on, she also gathers pollen—the yellow, powdery stuff that makes my nose run and my eyes itch. The pollen gets stored in her pollen baskets or just sticks to the little furry hairs on her body."

He squinted at notes scribbled into the margins. "The bee, covered with pollen from the anther, now moves on to the female part, the stigma, of the same flower or maybe another flower, and keeps digging for nectar. During the foraging, pollen falls off into the stigma, and whammo! The two plants have mated." He beamed. It's as though he has just pollinated a whole garden by himself, Sam thought.

Ms. Carlisle elaborated: "You described pollination," she said. "Once the flower is pollinated, the pollen generates a tube from the stigma to the ovary and fertilizes an egg, which begins the formation of a seed. We call this second step 'fertilization.'" Matt wrote it down.

"Ella." Ms. Carlisle was clearly not a person who wasted time. "You're up. What are we going to learn about?"

"In a word, or rather two words, colony collapse," Ella said. In 2006, beekeepers started noticing that their honeybees were dying off by the thousands or simply vanishing, leaving behind hives that, without any worker bees to sustain them, eventually collapsed. "Beekeepers reported hive losses as high as 40% or more, with some people estimating ..."

Ms. Carlisle abruptly held up her hand. "Now is a good time for me to stop you, summarize what I think your project is about, and suggest a framework for carrying it through."

The project has two main parts, she said. First, the study of bees and their role in pollination, and second, the threat to the environment that is known as Colony Collapse Disorder. "CCD is the most interesting part because it is current, relevant and remains, at this point, an unsolved mystery. So you need to approach it using the scientific process."

A pause. "For example, define your topic, collect and analyze relevant data, run experiments to test your hypotheses, form conclusions and finally, present your results." She waited for a response. "And remember to keep asking questions along the way. Start now. Ella?"

Ella was ready: "Okay, here's an obvious one: What is CCD? I can elaborate in the report. Next question: What do scientists and beekeepers think causes CCD? I can go into the different theories: It's caused by pesticides, it's caused by the lack of diversity in crops and wildflowers, it's caused by creepy intruders, like the parasitic varroa mites that suck out a bee's blood and bring viruses into the hive. I guess the question would be: 'Which of these, and others I haven't mentioned, result in the most damage, and why?'"

"Very good, Ella," Ms. Carlisle said. "Now let someone else speak."

That turned out to be Sam: "Maybe we should look at how big a problem CCD is. For example, does it just affect bees and beekeepers in New York State, or is it the whole country, even the whole planet?"

Tristan chimed in: "And who, besides the honeybee, is most affected by colony collapse?"

Ms. Carlisle nodded. "State that differently. In other words, what is the impact of CCD on different stakeholders, such as chemical manufacturers, big commercial farmers, individual beekeepers, grocery stores, farmers' markets and consumers?"

She looked expectantly at Matt. "Wow, my turn already?" His eyes darted around the floor as if he expected the answers to float up out of the cracked tiles. "Okay, how about: What if all the bees ended up dying? Are there other ways all those trees and flowers could get pollinated? Like some sort of spray? And how would candy companies replace all the nuts in their candy bars?"

Ms. Carlisle looked intently at him, as if he were a giant worm under one of her dusty microscopes. "Consider reframing that question, Matthew. For example: What solutions to CCD have been proposed? How would you evaluate the validity of those solutions?"

Ella again: "What if we found something that maybe could save at least some of the bees? Some data point no one else had thought about?"

Ms. Carlisle: "Good. And if you did come up with a hypothesis, how would you test it?"

Sam: "We could show what steps we took to prove or disprove the effectiveness of our idea, right?"

Ms. Carlisle looked satisfied. "Yes, you're starting to think like scientists."

Sam gave the final report, briefly describing how the team planned to buy four hives, each with about 20,000 bees, how they hoped to get anywhere from fifty to a hundred pounds of honey by the end of summer, and how they needed to raise enough money to pay for the bees, the hives, the protective bee suits and other beekeeping equipment.

Ms. Carlisle nodded. "You have your work cut out for you. And I'm about to add to it. Just how," she asked, "do you plan to view these wonderful insects in their natural habitats? Not by watching videos or looking at pictures, I trust. What arrangements have you made for this part of your project?"

Silence.

"Well, then," she said, "here is a suggestion. Visit the Pennsylvania Apiary Center in Fairfield. I met one of the guides during a trip through the state last summer. Call him. You may use my name. I'm sure he will remember me"—she paused, looking warily at the team—"and set up a Saturday when he can take you around the hives and the gardens."

The Center, she added, is next to two farms owned by commercial beekeepers who make a living traveling around the country with hundreds of hives loaded onto flatbed trucks. The bees will be rented out to big agricultural farmers. "Because of colony collapse," she said, "these farmers no longer have enough bees in their own fields to pollinate their crops. And it's only going to get worse."

The meeting was over. "That's all," she announced. "I'll expect a progress report in the spring. Good luck."

Sam, just before retreating to the hallway with his teammates, turned and looked back at Ms. Carlisle. She sat completely still, hands folded, eyes straight ahead. Now that her role as stern project adviser was over, the hard exterior of her face had melted into what looked like—what, exactly? Regret? Disappointment? Sorrow? She's been abandoned down here by someone or something that suddenly uprooted her life and changed even the physical environment around her, he thought. Like what happened to me, except at least I'm at the top of a busy hotel, not in a nearly deserted basement.

"You guys go ahead," he said to his friends, ignoring their surprise. "I'll catch up with you later."

Matt waved. "If you become an official missing person, we'll send a search party. Wouldn't want to find your little shriveled skeleton decades from now lying on Carlisle's floor."

Sam stood there, uncertain as to why he had held back, except that he would have liked to ask her about all those musty, messy things clustered in the corners, spilling off the desks, hanging from the walls—things she had refused to throw away despite their age. But where would he begin? And what would she say when she looked up and saw him staring, fumbling for words? He tiptoed away from the door and ran quickly down the hall after his friends.

Chapter 13

The Scary Big Number

"Money." Sam looked at his team as they sat around the table in his living room. "I get what Armand was talking about. Listen to what I found." He opened his notebook and began reading off a list of items:

The hive: "It comes with two deeps—the large boxes that go on the bottom of the hive—and two supers, the thinner, lighter boxes that go on top, plus forty frames. The frames are where the bees store their excess honey in tiny cells capped off with wax. Then a bottom board and two covers. Total cost for each hive: $225. Since we want four hives, that comes to $900."

The nuc: "It's short for nucleus, but it's pronounced 'nuke.' It's a small hive used to start a new colony, and it comes with a queen, lots of bees, and five frames already partially filled out with honey and pollen. And also with brood – that's what they call young bees in different stages of development, beginning with their life as an egg. When the frames fill out even more, we drop them into the regular hive box. Nucs, with any luck, will give us a jump start so we have at least a chance of actually getting some honey beginning in July. But they're expensive. Each nuc costs about $125. Times four is $500."

The extractor: "It's a small device that uses centrifugal force—Tristan can explain what that means later—to spin the honey from the cells and turn it into a liquid. The liquid flows into a container, ready to eat. We should get a hand-cranked one. It's the cheapest kind: $150."

Protective bee suit: It comes with mesh hat, veil, gloves, and a coverall with elastic at the ankles and wrists "so we don't get stung once we become official beekeepers and start hanging around what I hope will be 80,000 bees," Sam said. "Each complete suit costs about $100, times four is $400."

Smoker with leather bellows: "It calms the bees so that we can go in and collect the honey." Forty dollars.

Hive tool: "It pries apart frames that are stuck together with wax and propolis—what people call 'bee glue'—used by bees to seal open spaces in the hive." Ten dollars.

Sam sat back. "Phew. That's it. I'm almost afraid to ask what it all adds up to."

Tristan didn't seem to share that fear. "Exactly $2,000," he said promptly. "And that's probably a low estimate because—no offense, Sam—I'm sure there will be costs you haven't thought of. I mean, it's not like we know what we're doing."

Ella made a loud fizzing sound. "I feel like our hot air balloon has just been hit by a giant dart. I guess we never really thought about the money angle. And the committee didn't bring it up when they approved our proposal. They probably just don't know much about bees."

She repeated the alarming number: "$2,000. If we keep saying it, maybe it won't sound so big." The number actually sounded bigger. "The school gives each team $200 towards the cost of materials and other things," she added. "That won't even cover one hive. We need some ideas."

Silence, until Matt suddenly jolted upright in his armchair. "I got it! A bake sale! Cookies, cakes, brownies, muffins, raffle tickets! Winners get a free cooking class with one of the city's finest pastry chefs or maybe a cake in whatever shape they want." He hesitated. "Sam, would your dad go for that? I mean it's all for a good cause— us."

Sam pulled up his calendar. "We're in luck. The sports teams' bake sale is Tuesday, March 23, the week we're back from spring break. We can get permission to set up a table near them, and then we can ask Dad to help us make a list of the ingredients we'll need. Maybe he'll let us use Bella Vista's kitchen the weekend before so we can get a lot of the baking done ahead of time. This all just might work out."

Sam had more to report. Using a free, online application form, he had gotten permission from the Department of Health and Mental Hygiene to set up the hives. As part of the deal, beekeepers were required to follow appropriate practices, "which means we have to make sure our bees don't get in the way of pedestrians or people who live nearby. I doubt that will be a problem. We'll be sixteen stories off the ground. Not a lot of foot traffic up there. Also, we're not supposed to abandon the hives."

"Let just hope they don't abandon *us*," Tristan said. He looked around at the group. "It's kind of scary, isn't it? We know almost nothing about bees, and we're about to become beekeepers. It's like jumping out of an airplane and finding out you never got instructions on how to open your parachute."

Ella nodded at him. "You're right. We don't even know what we don't know. Maybe that's a good thing. Ignorance is underrated."

Matt and Tristan left for home, with Ella close behind. She

turned back at the door to wave at Sam, just in time to see him put his hands over his head and lean down over the living room table.

"Okay, Sam, what's up?" she said, coming back in and sitting next to him on the couch. "You're doing a surprisingly good imitation of a soccer goalie who just let in the tie-breaking goal."

Sam ignored the unpleasantly familiar image. "It's the bees," he said. "The thing is, once we have them, we're committed. We can't just return them to the delivery guy. We have to make sure we have the hives built and all the equipment we need."

And then, he went on, "Let's say everything works out, and it's September and the contest is over and winter is coming. Are we prepared to do whatever it takes to get the bees through the winter? And what about next spring? Will we do this all over again? Are we in this for life? Or are we the kind of bad people who abandon their hives when they get tired of being beekeepers?"

Ella got up to leave. "I don't have the answers, Sam. Maybe we could put it to the team. Look how far we've come already, and none of us are exactly bee experts, or money experts or anything experts. We'll make it work. Trust me."

Sam slumped back into the couch. He had been imagining a happy ending for everyone except, he now realized, one very important stakeholder—the tiny creatures that everyone was counting on to be the stars of the show.

Chapter 14

Facetime with a Pie

The table was set up. The baked goods they had prepared over the weekend, with help from Nick, Miguel, and The Meadows' kitchen, were wrapped and ready. Now all they needed were customers.

Sam glanced around the big atrium where student groups were already offering drinks, soft pretzels, bagels, tee shirts, and other items. I'm a terrible salesman, he thought. I should be standing here pushing all this great food, calling attention to the raffles, telling people these are the best pastries they'll find anywhere in the city.

"Step right up!" he suddenly heard Matt yelling over his shoulder. "You will never, ever, I mean never, get brownies, cookies, pies, pastries, and cakes as good as these! Brought to you all the way from New York's finest restaurant, offered here at bargain prices to people who are *ass-tute* enough to recognize quality when they see it! And," his voice rose higher, "for a modest amount of money, you can order a cake baked in any shape and flavor you want—for your birthday, for someone else's birthday, or just to pig out on all by yourself. So … who'll be the first to buy?"

Sam, Ella, and Tristan stared at him. Who would have thought that Matt could gather all his unfocused energy into a riveting speech about cookies and cherry pie?

Alex, a classmate from Sam's Spanish class, walked tentatively up to the table. "Good move, my man." Matt looked at him like a hawk sizing up a mouse. "What will it be? Cannoli? Macadamia nut cookie? Extra fudge brownie? A whole pie to get you through algebra?" Alex settled for two cookies.

"Time to celebrate our first sale," Matt said, stuffing half a brownie in his mouth just as two girls walked up to ask about the cakes. Matt handed an imaginary baton to Sam.

"Uh, what are you interested in?" Sam asked, his voice slightly cracking. Response: "Well, what are our choices?" Sam: "Well, we can have whatever you think you might want."

Matt hip checked Sam to one side. "What's the occasion? What can we help you celebrate?" His voice boomed out, as if the party, whatever it was, had already begun.

The occasion was a best friend's birthday, and the choice was a cake in the shape of a designer handbag that approximately half the girls in the seventh grade wore like it was a third arm. Matt looked over to Sam: "This should be a piece of cake for your father, right?"

By now a small crowd was gathering in front of the table. Sam no longer had time to think about his failure as a salesman. While Matt and Ella sold the pastries and raffles and took cake orders, he and Tristan kept bringing up more food from the boxes underneath. We might actually pull this off, Sam thought. Queen bees, hives, road trip—we're on our way.

"What's that?" Matt pointed to a group of kids on the opposite side of the atrium. Four of them were setting up a table, music was suddenly blasting out of a laptop, and the crowd in front of The Bee Team's table started to slowly drift away.

"It's Reed and company," said Ella. "I'd heard they were going to have a sale to raise money. But at the same time in the same place as ours? That's just slimy."

"Exactly what are they selling?" Matt asked, straining to see above the students milling around the other table. Ella and Sam strolled casually over to check it out.

"Whoa," Sam said to Ella. "What *aren't* they selling." One section of the table offered Charlene's "expert manis" next to a poster showing perfectly manicured fingers with bright purple and red nail polish.

"Yeah, like I would ever let Charlene within five feet of any part of my body," Ella whispered.

Standing over another section, Reed held up a shaver and promised to shave his head if students donated "enough money to make it worth my while." "Brilliant," sighed Ella. "A lot of people would like to see Reed's head get smaller."

The third section sold coupons that entitled purchasers to attend a pre-screening of a first-run movie, title not yet released. "Miles' mother works somewhere in the entertainment industry," said Ella, tilting her head towards Miles, who was busy waving piles of coupons at the crowd.

Back at The Bee Team table, it looked as though someone had detonated a stink bomb. "They knew exactly what they were doing, setting up to compete directly in our space," fumed Matt. "I'd say this means war."

Tristan did the accounting: "We've sold less than half our food and exactly twelve raffle tickets. It's not as though these baked goods can be stored for another day. We need to come up with something, fast."

"Okay, time for the hard sell," said Matt, rubbing his hands together, "and that means we take no prisoners. We hit them where it hurts. We go right for the jugular." He was beginning to run out of clichés.

Sam leaned towards Ella: "I'm glad he's on our side... I think."

"Just what do you mean by 'jugular?'" Ella asked Matt, but he was already moving into the center of the big hallway and starting his windup.

"Hey, everyone," he shouted out. "While you watch Reed get his head flattened, you will want to munch on our cookies, cakes, pies, and everything else, and they won't last long. Same for our raffle tickets—a chance to win a free cooking lesson from one of the best pastry chefs in New York. For everyone but you, those classes cost hundreds and thousands of dollars. Here, you get a chance at them for almost nothing. Impress your friends. Impress your parents..."

While he talked, he broke off big chunks of a double chocolate cookie and ate each one very slowly. I can almost taste them, Sam thought. This guy is a natural.

Matt had only just begun. Finishing off the cookie, he began slowly moving to the music of the robot team's boom box and, even more slowly, pulling off his sweatshirt, then twirling it above his head, over his shoulders, across his butt, and onto the floor. The tee shirt was next. He swirled and dipped, extending one arm at a time to pull each sleeve off. Another twirl and the tee shirt was flung across the atrium, landing precariously on the robot team table before slipping onto the floor.

"Is Matt really doing a striptease?" Sam asked Ella and Tristan. "And where did he get those moves?" More dips and swirls, and then the undershirt. Both arms reached down to pull it slowly up over his head, then off and out into the crowd. The audience, at first too stunned to move, began to clap to the music, a chorus of catcalls—"Take it all off" was the loudest—rising from all sides.

Matt smiled and began to remove his belt, all the while edging closer to The Bee Team table. Belt off, time now for the jeans. Ella looked at Sam. "He really can't go any further. Can he?"

Tristan was studying the crowd reaction. "I think this is what they mean by 'stage presence.'"

Matt's boxer shorts made a brief appearance just as two science teachers, including Ms. Hineline, entered the atrium. She marched up to Matt: "What on earth are you doing?" she shouted above the music.

"I'm selling," he said, grabbing his shirts and putting them on faster than Sam had ever seen anyone get dressed. "But I'm done. Would you like to buy a cookie?" She didn't. And she didn't want to see any more of Matt's striptease, ever.

Meanwhile, the tide had turned. Students were once again congregating around The Bee Team table. "I'm not sure how long we can keep their attention," Sam said. "But at least we're back in the game."

Ella nudged Sam: "Reed looks furious, and I think he's heading over here."

Reed strutted up to The Bee Team. "A bake sale," he said loudly. "How quaint. Are you selling candy hearts too? And teddy bears? I would've thought The Bee Team could come up with something a little more twenty-first century, a little more imaginative, but I guess that's why you're not The A Team."

"Oops," Sam said out loud. Not a good move. He could see what looked like hives, not the bee kind, creeping up over Matt's face.

But Reed hadn't finished. "And I bet the robots we're building could bake better pies than the ones you're selling."

"You think so?" Matt practically spit the words out. "Here, taste one and let me know." He picked up a cherry pie and squashed it squarely into Reed's face.

The crowd of students froze, hypnotized by the sight of gooey red filling and flaky crust clinging, like a mud pack, to the contours of Reed's face, all except for two hollowed out circles around his eyes. Dozens of cell phone cameras clicked, several students began to laugh, and Sam rushed up to Reed with a bunch of paper towels.

"Well," said Tristan. "That's one pie we're not going to be able to sell."

Chapter 15

Point of No Return

Approximately twenty-four hours later, the results were in. Tristan, leaning against the couch in Sam's living room, announced the total: "$462, minus the $60 we owe your dad for the ingredients."

Matt let out a long whistle: "Not bad! It was all those raffle tickets! How many did we sell?"

Tristan checked his numbers: "Exactly 96, plus seven cakes, four pies and more than a hundred cookies, brownies and muffins. No Rice Krispie treats, Matt, because you ate all ten of them."

Sam pumped his fist: "We beat our goal by $102! A lot of it was because of you, Matt. You were great. Sorry you have to buy Reed a new sweatshirt. And then there's all that community service. Fifty hours? Wow, that's up there. But the pictures everyone took will live on forever. You're already a Manhattan School for Science legend."

"Not in everyone's eyes," Ella said. "Just want you to know that Reed and the others were glaring and pointing and whispering the whole day. I bet they're thinking serious payback."

"Just what could they do to us?" Matt looked skeptical. "Every teacher is on the lookout for more trouble. Even my parents are giving me the evil eye. I might as well have a big red P on my shirt. For 'Pie.'" He grinned. "But I'm definitely lying low, at least for now. So Sam, what are we doing with $402?"

Sam called up a website. "I think we should go ahead and order our nucs and hives. We can get the nucs from an apiary in New Jersey and the hives from a company in Illinois. The tricky thing is we need to pay them the money now, about $1,400, in order to get all this by early April. We can count on $200 from the school, but no matter how you add it up, we're still way short."

Armand, he reminded the team, wasn't going to okay the use of the room until he knew how everything would be paid for. "He doesn't want a half-finished mess left on the roof. Any ideas?"

No one spoke up. "Okay, here's one," Sam said. "So, Armand, Elaine and Simon want to make sure we have enough money, right? How about if we suggest doing a bunch of chores around the hotel in return for a donation? They'd be getting something concrete, and we wouldn't just be sitting around on our hands waiting for the money to magically appear."

"What are you thinking we would do?" Matt asked. "Lick some bowls? Ice some cupcakes? Taste test new recipes?"

Sam looked disgusted until he realized Ella was laughing. "Oh, I get it. You're kidding. Hard to tell sometimes. Maybe we could paint some rooms or clean out storage areas, maybe move furniture around… I don't know. It would be whatever they dream up."

Sam made a list: Work out a plan and show it first to Nick. Answer Armand's questions about the permits and the amount of honey the bees will produce. Deliver the plan to Armand's assistant. Wait for the verdict. Assume it's "yes." If it's not, lock yourself in your room and don't come out for a year.

"You know, we're becoming like the bees, doing whatever it takes for the good of the hive," Ella said. "Which means that if one of us—picture a particularly large drone—isn't pulling his weight..." She glanced at Matt. "The rest of us will have to join forces and kick his useless butt off the roof. Efficiency rules, right?"

****

Sam felt as though he was entering an alien universe with none of the powers that guide superheroes through the unknown. It was time to order the bees and beehives. "Okay, everybody look over what I've done and see if you can find any mistakes," he said, one sweaty hand clutching a credit card co-signed by his father. Nick had agreed to loan the team enough money to cover its first two purchases.

Matt, Ella, and Tristan moved closer to the computer in Sam's bedroom. "So we decided to order four nucs, right?" Sam pointed to the screen. "And we agreed to buy them from the Joseph Langstroth Apiary in Basking Ridge, New Jersey, right?"

And get them delivered. When Sam had explained to the Langstroth beekeeper that four middle school kids were getting the nucs as part of a science project, he had agreed to bring them to the hotel—and pick them up once they were no longer needed—in return for six cannoli, one mocha buttercream cake, and a dozen small apple tarts. "He said he came into Manhattan twice a week anyway. And he had heard of Bella Vista. So I doubt this is much of a hardship."

Sam didn't tell the team about his colossal, heroic, unprecedented sacrifice—all for the good of the team. In return for Nick providing pastries for the beekeeper, Sam had agreed to make his own bed, *and* Nick's, for the next *month*.

On to the hives. "We're ordering four hive kits, right? Each one has two deep brood boxes and a medium depth super already assembled, one metal cover, one inner cover, one entrance reducer—that helps prevent robber bees from coming in to steal the honey and also prevents mice from eating the stored pollen and making a big mess in the winter—one entrance feeder, the screened bottom board, and one hive tool. Plus a queen excluder. That's a barrier to make sure the queen lays her eggs inside the deep and not higher up in the supers where surplus honey is stored."

He went on: "Here's where it gets more interesting. Each hive kit includes forty frames plus foundation imprinted with the shapes of hexagonal cells. We'll have to assemble those ourselves. How hard can that be?"

Last items, on hold for now: "We'll get the bee suits, hats, gloves, smoker, all that, in our next order," Sam said. He pushed the "buy" button on two different sites.

Ella looked at the team. "You know that famous phrase, 'On the internet nobody knows you're a dog?' Well, for our purposes, nobody knows we're a bunch of seventh graders ordering hundreds of dollars of equipment even though we don't know the first thing about beekeeping. Anonymity has its uses."

Chapter 16

Baseball Turns Ugly

Baseball practice, three p.m., in the small park two blocks away from the Manhattan School for Science, a beautiful spring afternoon that drew a bunch of student spectators happy to trade seats in the computer lab for seats on the field's rickety bleachers.

"Tristan doesn't exactly look like an all-star," Ella whispered to Sam as they sat in the bleachers watching Tristan and the others warm up.

"Yeah, I don't think sports are really his thing," said Sam. "In fact, I'm pretty sure he hates them in any form. Put him in a dungeon with peanut butter crackers, apple juice, and a laptop, and he'd be fine."

Tristan, Sam noticed, was on the same side as Reed, playing third base while Reed was at shortstop. I have a bad feeling about this, he thought, watching Reed furtively size up Tristan out of the corner of his eye, as if calculating the shortest distance between the two.

One minute later, a player on the at-bat side sent a ball sailing over third base heading to the outfield. At the last moment, it began to curve, looking like it would end up in foul ball territory. Tristan moved, glove arm held high. Reed had the same idea, running hard on a sideways course that would take him directly into Tristan's path.

Everyone on and off the field held their breath. Just close your eyes, and you won't see the train wreck you know is coming, Sam told himself. In fact, he couldn't stop watching, couldn't help but see Reed raise his elbow and collide full speed into Tristan, sending him crashing into the bleachers, but not just into the bleachers, into a big wooden box filled with balls and bats that scattered on impact over several rows of seats. Reed held up his glove, with the ball nestled smack in the middle, and grinned. "You're out," he shouted at the batter, and then turned to look at Tristan. Sam imagined he could see Reed whisper the words, "And you're out, too."

The players nearest the bleachers untangled Tristan from the equipment that lay in a heap around him. The third base coach yelled for someone to call an ambulance, and almost immediately one showed up, roaring onto the field, sirens blaring.

Sam watched as Tristan was lifted onto a stretcher and loaded into the back of the ambulance. He turned and saw Reed put an arm around Charlene and saunter off the field, both of them grinning like co-conspirators celebrating the overthrow of a pesky rival.

The smiles on their faces did it. Sam ran up and slammed his fist into Reed's chest, feeling a sharp pain in his thumb as it made contact, feeling his rage almost blind him to the target, feeling the punch slide off Reed's sweatshirt. Not much of a blow, but Reed appeared stunned, dumbfounded, clearly unused to being the victim instead of the attacker.

And then suddenly Matt was there, his own fists clenched, standing next to Sam. "Come on, Reed," he said softly. "Take a swing. The coaches aren't looking. I dare you. Or does this just prove that you're too chicken to take on someone your own size?"

Reed moved a few steps backward. "You're not worth it," he hissed. "Watch me. I'm leaving before you get seriously hurt. Say hi to Tristan. Tell him he needs to work on his catching."

****

Shiner: a circle of bright black that fades to yellow greenish and then to nothing. Tristan's black eye was in the second, yellow-green stage.

He was perched on the edge of his bed, turning to the light as Sam and Matt both leaned over to take a closer look. Ella sat down next to him. "Not bad. Not as gross as I thought," she said. "I guess you're lucky. Both your eyes could have been jabbed instead of just one."

"Lucky?" Tristan echoed. "That's not a word I would have chosen. The rib is okay. The crack will heal by itself, and it doesn't hurt much as long as I don't breathe deeply, or laugh. No chance of that."

"Yes, but consider this," Sam said. "At the very least, you're getting excused from sports for the rest of the semester. And I'm sure you heard about Reed." Tristan hadn't. "He's suspended from the junior varsity team, which is pretty drastic because the senior varsity is usually fielded from the J.V."

Tristan managed a weak smile, then pointed silently to the cast on his left hand that covered the area above his wrist to just below the tips of his fingers. It was a light grayish color, and the fingertips looked waxy, like they had been stored overnight in soapy water. Even a week for someone who practically lives on his laptop is a very long time, Sam thought. I'm not going to ask when the cast comes off.

"I've got another four weeks, at least, with this cast." Tristan clearly had mind-reading powers. "That's the worst part. I mean, the black eye and the rib—those are nothing. But I'm missing out on a lot of the programming class. Once you fall behind, you might as well drop out."

Matt squinted at the cast. "Tristan, listen. If you can't manage the typing, I could come with you to your class and be like, you know, your own private *ste-nog-ra-pher*. I won't have any idea what they're talking about, but at least I can input things. I'm pretty fast. Not sure about the accuracy, but it's probably better than nothing."

Tristan shook his head. "We're solving problems as we're inputting, so you have to think and move fast, and the data builds on itself really quickly. But just talking about it makes me think I can probably do a lot with one hand."

Matt, after the attack of the cherry pie, knows he should have been the target of Reed's revenge, Sam thought. But that would have been too risky for Reed. It's so much easier to take on someone thirty pounds lighter. And Tristan's broken wrist? Matt's offer of help surprised him, Sam decided. It kind of surprised *me*. Maybe all our talk about bees' incredible teamwork, and the way they always pull together for the good of the hive, is rubbing off on him.

Matt moved over to Tristan's bed and gave him an awkward pat on the back. "Okay, I have to go. But I'm here if you need anything. And don't worry about Reed. He's going to be sorry he pushed, *flung*, you into the bleachers. Like that guy said, 'I've not yet begun to fight.'"

Sam looked around the room as Matt was leaving. "Nice place," he said to Tristan before he realized there were no posters, banners, or pictures on any of the walls or surfaces—just long, blank expanses of white, with one exception. Almost hidden behind the lamp on a bedside table was a photo of a woman who looked exactly like Tristan.

Ella held it up, her eyes moving back and forth from Tristan to the photo. "Do I even need to guess who this is?" She put it down in front of the lamp. "You look just like her."

"Yeah, it's my mother," Tristan said. "She lives in Los Angeles, which means I don't get to see her much, almost never, but we talk on the phone once in a while when my Dad isn't home. To say he's angry with her is an understatement. I think I understand why. I mean she just got up one day, packed a few bags, and left. She said he wasn't ambitious enough for her or something like that. So why did they ever get married in the first place?"

Tristan looked as though he actually expected Sam to answer that question. *He feels the same emptiness that I have felt first thing every morning for the last fourteen months,* Sam thought, *like there is this huge gash in my chest that hurts until I make myself imagine it closing up, even though I know it's not really closing, because right now I can't see it ever healing, ever letting me go.*

Sam looked at the photo again. "Tristan, Ella, listen. I need to tell you something, although you probably already know. Maybe *everybody* knows, even though no one, not even you guys, has ever asked me about it, about what happened and why we moved to New York and why it's just Dad and me living alone in an apartment at the top of a hotel. Maybe you just guessed that something bad brought us here, and thought I should be the one to bring it up, to talk about it. So here, I'm talking about it."

He sat down on the other side of Tristan. "We moved after my mother died in a car accident. At eleven p.m., January 5." He stopped to catch his breath. "In about five seconds, everything turned upside down, without any warning, nothing to say this night was going to be different from all the others. She was coming home from her and Dad's restaurant, and a car driving the wrong way hit her head-on. The other person hadn't even slowed down."

His sentences were running together, but the rush of words felt good—memories finally spoken and shared instead of buried. "My dad didn't wake me up until the morning, after he came back from the hospital. She had died in the ambulance on the way there, but he wanted to tell me when it was daytime. I mean as if daylight would change the fact that I would never see her again."

He looked out the window. "All I wanted at that moment was to go wherever she was so that I could take care of her, like she had always taken care of me. Because, you know, there were things she couldn't do well. Like she had a terrible sense of direction. We were always getting lost driving to our away games, and in winter, the zipper on her down jacket was always getting stuck and I would have to pull the fabric out and thread it down and get it back up on the track. We would be laughing the whole time and she would hug me and call me the fastest zipper-man in the East. And she could never remember the soccer coach's name. I had to remind her every time she dropped me off.... That night, why couldn't there have been just one last moment with her when I could have said goodbye?"

He knew that tears were dripping onto his shirt. He felt Ella's hand reach across Tristan and take his own, and he sensed, maybe he heard, that she was crying, too.

Out of the corner of his eye, he saw Tristan, his face panic-stricken, looking at the wall, his cast, his closet door. And then, finally, he looked at Sam. "I'm sorry about your mother. I don't know what I would do if there wasn't even the possibility of seeing mine again. I just figure she's storing up some time, and then she'll come back into my life. I'm not sure how, but that's for her to figure out. She's the one who left, right?"

"Sam! Ella!" Ron, Tristan's father, called from somewhere in the apartment. "Can you wrap it up? Tristan needs to get some rest."

"Got it!" Sam shouted back, wiping his face with the back of his hand.

Ella got up and blew her nose. "Sam, it wasn't hard to figure out that something awful had happened, and that it probably had to do with your mom. Every once in a while, you would just disappear, even though you were sitting right next to me, or we were all up on the roof together. I knew you were sad, but you never wanted to talk about it. So I never asked. It wasn't that I didn't care. I hope you know that. I have always cared."

Tristan got off the bed and stood next to Ella. He's expressing solidarity, in his own silent way, Sam said to himself, feeling a sudden rush of gratitude that they were his friends.

Time to move on. Sam took some homework folders out of his backpack. "Ella helped me pull together a lot of this stuff so that you wouldn't get too far behind," he said to Tristan. "Besides, we need you. Our team can't afford any slacker bees, especially smart ones. If the competition thought you weren't fully committed, they would start calling us The Cee Team."

Tristan laughed for a split second before he stopped abruptly and laid his hand over his rib. "I'm okay," he said. "The pain was worth it. And yeah, so what I've been doing while I've been at home is working on a design for a new kind of hive that I saw described in an article about two Australian beekeepers." He pulled out a diagram that had different sketches of beehives, with little "x"es drawn in for the bees. "Maybe at some point I could use the 3-D printer at Columbia to show you what it really looks like."

Ella lightly tapped Tristan's chest, and Sam offered a soft high-five. "Keep working on the 3-D hive," Ella said. "It could put us over the top. If the Evil Ones win, they'll throw it in our faces for the next six years."

That assumes I'm here for the next six years, or even one more year, Sam thought, as he walked with Ella down the stairs of the building and onto the street. Make that not even six months. If The Meadows' bosses lose patience and too much money, Nick might be out of a job as early as the fall.

Chapter 17

The Big Cleanup

The first truly sunny Saturday of spring, and here I am cleaning a toilet bowl in the basement of The Meadows, Sam thought, wiping a piece of green crud off his forearm. The Bee Team's memo had worked. Armand had approved the use of the hotel's roof and agreed to hire the team for a day of what Armand's return memo had labeled "heavy labor."

He called out to Ella: "I knew that sounded bad. I didn't think painting involved scrubbing and sanding, or that cleaning would include digging out bathroom fixtures covered with grime and mildew and dead bugs and other stuff I don't even want to think about."

Ella appeared out of the big storage closet next to the bathroom, her hair in one long braid that hung down her back, her hands in thick, grey, oversized work gloves, huge cobwebs crisscrossing her sweatshirt and sweat pants. "They warned us. These areas haven't been cleaned for months. The plan must be to get them ready in case the hotel ever needs more storage space."

Matt walked in with paint, a small stepladder, plaster, three brushes, sandpaper, rollers, and under his arm, a plastic sheet. He took one look at Ella and let out a long whistle. "The Midtown Mummy gets down and dirty. We should never have skipped the Halloween party. Can you save those cobwebs for next year? And maybe that creepy little spider crawling up your leg?" Ella quickly began swatting at her sweatpants, alternately stomping and shaking each leg. No spider in sight.

"Ell!" said Sam. "Matt's teasing you. There aren't any spiders. Maybe a few stinkbugs, and phew, a lot of giant cockroaches…"

She stopped swatting, delivered her best drop-dead-morons look, then took aim at Matt. "Did you oversleep, Matt? Are you still trying to figure out how to set your Mickey Mouse alarm clock?"

Matt waved away the question, focusing instead on unloading all the equipment onto the floor in one big, disorganized pile. "So how much are we getting paid for this?" he asked.

"Unclear," said Sam. "Dad told me that if the hotel made the arrangement an official transaction, it would be breaking some labor laws. Instead, they can give us a 'tip' depending on how much we do. So let's get on with it. It's going to be a long day."

The team divided the chores into five parts: removing wallpaper, cleaning, plastering, painting, and last on the list, clearing out a huge collection of furniture on the top floor, moving some to the trash area behind the hotel and the rest to the basement.

"This is worse than I thought," Matt said, looking at the vast expanse of hallway with its pock-marked plaster and peeling wallpaper. "At least they had the paint ready for us. Lucky Tristan. I wouldn't have minded cracking a rib right around now. Except that I know how much you both would have missed me." He smiled and batted his eyelids.

Sam offered to act as foreman of the crew, assigning and setting up chores in the right order.

Ella suddenly glared at him. "So glad you're taking the lead. What would we do without you? How would we function if you didn't hand out the jobs, show us how to do them, when to do them, where to do them, tell us when we can take breaks, when we can go home. We would be lost without you, Sam."

Sam put down his toilet brush and walked over to Ella. "Okay. I get it. You guys think I like ordering people around. I don't. I just want to make sure everything gets done, and done really well, because otherwise, what's the point? We would just turn in a stupid, boring science project, and I would lose my scholarship and everything else." He turned to face Ella. "So you do it. You organize us." He slumped down against the wall.

After one very long moment of silence, Ella squatted next to him. "Sorry," she whispered, moving her body closer to his so that the top of her shoulder lightly brushed his arm. "I guess I'm already sick of this job. Sick of the science project, and Charlene, and worrying about what Reed will do next, and who he will do it to. How about if we take a short break? Matt, I know you just arrived, but do you think you could manage a quick snack?"

In the elevator, standing behind Matt, she took Sam's hand. Even covered with cobwebs and dressed in a baggier sweatshirt than usual, she was breath-taking—loose strands of plastered-down hair like golden veins along her neck, flecks of paint glittering like tiny diamonds on her forehead. He laced his fingers through hers and wished the elevator ride was three times as long or that it would get stuck between floors and that Matt would somehow disappear.

None of this happened. Snack over, they spent the next three hours scouring the bathroom and storage area, stripping wallpaper, sandpapering, and re-plastering. Then lunch in the hotel kitchen, and another four hours of painting doors, walls, and window trims, lugging furniture around, and cleaning up.

By five p.m., they were ready to move the last, beat-up old chest into the storage room. Once it had been settled in a corner, Ella pried open the top drawer to see what was rattling around. A small box decorated with tiny hand-painted flowers and birds skidded to the front. "It looks like it's really old. Not just old. Ancient. Like maybe from a hundred years ago."

She pulled out a few note cards and held them up to the hanging bulb in the ceiling. On the front of each, written in very stylish script with curling capital letters and little squiggles between sentences, were names and addresses. Matt read some of the names out loud: "Sophie Vanderbilt, Sarah Astor, Helen Gould, Frances Morgan, Adelaide Frick, Mary Harriman, Laura Rockefeller. Who *are* these people?"

Ella grabbed his arm: "Wait a minute. I think I just might know…" She ran through some searches on her phone. "Yes! These were society women from the nineteenth century, and they were married to some of the richest people in New York—the bankers, the railroad guys, the oil men."

She flipped over a few of the cards. "Each one has a recipe on the back. I wonder if these women were part of a social club, and at one point, they all contributed recipes for some specific purpose. Maybe to create a cookbook? Or to give out as gifts? Or maybe just to share with each other's cooks? Because I'm sure they didn't do any of the cooking and cleaning themselves. But for some reason, this box never got given out, and it ended up stored in this chest."

Sam squinted at a recipe on one of the cards and let out a shout. "It's for Honey Taffy!" He quickly turned over another card. The top line read, "Bee Sting Cake." Other recipes offered "Baked Sticky Honey Chicken," "Skillet Honey Beef," "Raw Honey Tea and Biscuits," and something called "Shrub."

Ella kept staring at the box. "This is a goldmine," she whispered. "Do you get what this could do for our science project? And for the restaurant? Sam, your dad can actually make these recipes with the honey we produce." Her voice rose as more ideas tumbled out. "And we can display each one and look up more about the women who donated them. Luckily for us, honey seems to have been a very popular ingredient."

****

By early evening, the crew was sprawled out on the couch and chairs in Sam's living room, the box stowed in the bottom of his desk.

Ella pulled herself into a sitting position. "Okay, I've got it! We put each recipe on a notecard with the ingredients and cooking instructions on the front. On the back we add a brief sketch of the woman who donated it. Then maybe we attach a honey lollipop or some wrapped piece of honey candy, and we sell the notecards at the restaurant, at school, wherever. Armand splits the money with us, and we use it to pay back Sam's dad and cover any other bee expenses. It's brilliant."

Matt shot up off the couch and, in mid-air, began the waggle dance. "So you like it?" Ella deadpanned. "I wasn't sure."

She offered to get the recipe card production going and design a "company" logo. Matt volunteered the absent Tristan to help him visit novelty shops in Manhattan for ideas on pricing. Sam would work with the kitchen staff on how to best display the cards.

He leaned back into the soft cushions of the couch. "We all did a great job," he croaked, almost too exhausted to speak. "And next time I'll suggest a little easier way to make money. Like cleaning graffiti off the New York City subway system."

Matt repeated the question that had come up three times

since lunch. "So how much do you think they'll pay us? I mean, let's face it. We did an A+ job. We should get A+ money."

Ella was counting: "So three of us worked seven hours each, which means twenty-one hours. And don't we get paid for the lunch hour too? So twenty-four hours. If a professional painter or house cleaning crew was doing this, how much do you think they would charge an hour? Ten dollars? Fifteen? Twenty-five? Fifty?"

Sam did the math. "If we get paid ten dollars an hour, that's $240. Doesn't seem like much. If we get fifty dollars an hour, that's … $1,200. I have a feeling it's going to be closer to $240."

Cleanup time. Sam surveyed his teammates. "It looks like we got half the paint and plaster on ourselves. Wow guys, nice hair—the blue streaks and those matching blue blobs around your ears. Very cool."

Ella put a plaster-caked arm around his shoulder. "Sam, have you checked out a mirror recently? Those red paint smudges on your nose and neck, and forehead? They look like blood."

She leaned in so that her head was two inches from his, her eyes moving slowly, deliberately, lingeringly, from the top of his face down to the top of his chest. In any other situation, Sam thought to himself, trying not to breathe, this would be an incredibly warm, tender, intimate moment. He knew this was not going to be that moment. Ella gently traced the curve of one of his eyebrows. "Not very authentic, Sam. I don't think even Dracula would bite."

Chapter 18

Matt Saves the Day

They stared at the four boxes sitting on a big conference table in one of The Meadows' meeting rooms. The deeps and supers were there, already assembled, along with the bottom boards, entrance reducers, queen excluders, and inner and outer covers. But the frames were in pieces, sitting next to a tube of glue and a bunch of 1¼-inch nails. According to an instruction manual stuck to a crease in the bottom of the box, beekeepers needed to provide their own hammer, razor blade, and carpenter's square. "I feel like we've been given one of those tool boxes you get as a little kid and told to build a space station," said Tristan. "Where do we begin?"

Ella laid out all the parts. No one moved.

"We need to jumpstart ourselves," Matt suddenly announced. "I suggest some O.J. and maybe some cereal and pancakes. Sam, can we take a quick break?"

Why not, Sam thought. It's Saturday morning, we all got up earlier than usual, we're tired and yeah, we're intimidated. Definitely time to get juiced.

The breakfast dishes, including baskets of leftover muffins and croissants, were just coming back from the dining room. Miguel, halfway through an early morning shift, caught a glimpse of Matt barreling through the swinging doors. "Invader alert!" he called out, covering the baskets with his arms and chest. "Lock down the counters, raise the metal bars, call Seal Team Six …"

Matt was now inches from the baskets. "Very funny, Miguel. Here you have a chance to help four brilliant, young scientists complete a task so difficult and so important that the fate of the whole Western world hangs in the balance. But no, you're actually trying to do a cover-up, one that I might add is *few-tile*."

Miguel smiled: "Just what big task are you up to, Matt? Binge-watching reruns of your favorite cartoon show?"

Ella slid one of the muffin baskets out from under Miguel's arms. "It's the bees," she said. "We have one day—today—to assemble the hives, and I don't think any of us guessed how totally complicated it is. You should see what we've just unpacked! So many parts. And the instructions look like they're written in German."

Miguel held up both hands. "Hold on. You're telling me that you're having trouble building the hives? But it's easy! My father lives near Managua, in Nicaragua. He's kept hives on his property ever since I can remember. We never used those pre-made ones. We built the hives from nothing—just wood, metal, nails, and a few old tools. The big payoff was scraping the honey off the frames and spinning it. I had to wear a hat and long-sleeved shirt but my father wore nothing. He said his 'babies' would never sting him, and if they did, he would understand. After all, we were stealing from them, right? Nothing anywhere else in the world has ever tasted as good as that raw honey. Maybe that's where I got the idea that I wanted to be a chef."

Funny how bees play a role in so many people's lives, Sam thought. "Time to go," he said out loud. "It's our first big test as beekeepers. Let's ace it."

******

The Bee Team once again looked at the hive parts lying on the table. Sam had no idea where to find a carpenter's square, or what it was even used for. But he had managed to find a hammer and a razor blade.

Matt began to walk slowly around the table, shifting his attention back and forth between the instructions and the four pieces of wood that made up each frame—two side bars and a top and bottom bar. He used the razor blade to cut off little slivers of extra wood.

He picked up a side bar and carefully deposited a drop of glue in the groove carved out of its top, then took a top bar and fitted its notch into the groove. He repeated the process with the other side, fitting the notched end of the other top bar into the other groove. To complete the frame, he squeezed a small amount of glue onto the grooves in the bottom ends of the two side bars and carefully locked in the frame's bottom bar.

It's as if the rest of us aren't here, Sam thought. He's in total concentration mode, and he's actually looking at each page of the instruction book.

With the hammer, Matt nailed ten of the small nails into the bottom, top and side of the frame, occasionally holding it up to the light to make sure the right angles were squared correctly. A few more glances at the instruction book, a few more nails pounded into the frame, and that part of the job was done.

Matt didn't pause. He built a total of fourteen more frames and inserted them into the deeps.

"It's so compact," Tristan said softly, running his hands lightly over the exterior of one of the hives. "And efficient. Nothing's wasted here. All the different spaces serve a function."

Sam was impressed for a different reason: Matt has shape-shifted into a different person right before our eyes, he thought. It's like another human being, hidden beneath the clumsy, inarticulate one, has suddenly risen to the top.

"So why don't we divide up into teams of two," Matt suggested. "Sam and Tristan can work together, and Ella with me. Forget about speed. Just make sure that the right nails are in the right places, that the parts are correctly aligned, and that there's the right amount of space between the frames. We shouldn't feel like we're in a race."

Sam looked around at the group. "Matt uncompetitive? We're definitely in another dimension."

Matt and Ella attacked the project as though they had been building hives together for years. The nails went in straight, the glue went on smoothly, the frames were distanced correctly, and the different pieces fit squarely on top of each other.

But what's really amazing, Sam said to himself, is how intent they are, working head to head, anticipating each other's needs, offering advice with no sarcasm, no jokes. They haven't looked up once. Their concentration is like a force field around them, shutting out the rest of the room, shutting out me.

Ella heaped praise on her partner. "You're a pro, Matt. I mean you're a natural builder. You've made this great home for the bees. It's awesome."

Geez, enough already, Sam said to himself. It's just hives. You haven't built the Taj Mahal. It doesn't help that Tristan and I look like we're trying out for the Marx Brothers construction crew.

"One of your nails has gone in crooked," Matt said, coming over to look at the skewed bar-end alignment that represented about 15 minutes of effort by Sam and Tristan. "I'll remove it and you can try again." He took out the nail, adjusted the pieces and pounded the parts back in place.

That's how the rest of the construction went. Sam and Tristan built a frame, and Matt rebuilt it. They put the frames into the supers, and Matt took them out and re-inserted them. The only break in their rhythm was when they ran out of the hive boxes' commercial glue used to reinforce the corners. Production stopped while Sam dug out some homemade glue, a leftover from grade school, from an old tool chest in the hallway closet.

"Wow. 2 p.m. I'm famished," Matt suddenly announced. The spell was broken, Sam thought, except that normally Ella would have been baiting Matt with a joke about his cannoli addiction, his brownie habit, his stealth cookie raids. Instead, she smiled at Matt and actually took his arm. "Me, too. Let's go to the sub shop near your house. I'll buy you a double cheesesteak and chocolate shake."

Ella and Matt headed for the door. Sam called loudly after them: "Okay, guys, I'll go to the hardware store and get the paint. One gallon of primer and one gallon of what? What color should we get?"

The only response was from Tristan. "How about blue? And I'll go with you," he said. "I figured we might need a few more things for the hives, so I brought some money from our slush fund, the $200 we got from school."

Great, thought Sam. I'm paired with Tristan to buy paint, and those two are out getting lunch and celebrating their architectural brilliance. Matt and Ella? It didn't sound right.

****

It didn't sound any better twenty-four hours later. Sam sat on the couch in his living room staring at four fully assembled beehives on the floor next to the coffee table. They actually looked good. He and Tristan had spent part of the morning and afternoon applying three coats of bright blue paint, and the hives were now ready for action.

He went over, once again, how yesterday afternoon had turned out to be so dismal. He didn't mind, at least not that much, being shown up as a clumsy, incompetent hive builder. We can't all be good at everything, right? What was bad was how quickly The Bee Team had been reconfigured. Matt and Ella, strolling off arm in arm for cheesesteaks.

Even Miguel sensed that the afternoon had been weird, Sam knew. That morning in the kitchen, he had called out to him in one of those false-jovial voices that adults use when they are saying the opposite of what everyone knows to be true. "Hey, Sam. I heard the team pulled it off. The hives are ready for action! Good job!"

"Yeah, they're ready," Sam said, hunched so low over his cereal bowl that his nose was practically in the milk.

"Come on, Sam," Miguel shot back. "I know why you're down. Trust me, you don't need to be. I'm twice your age, but I can still read signals, even hidden ones. And there were lots of those yesterday. Apparently you missed them."

"Whatever, okay, I've got to study for some tests," Sam mumbled. "But thanks for whatever you said."

The afternoon dragged on: four p.m. and he was looking at more than four hours of homework. I need a crane to get me up off the couch, he thought, or maybe a fire drill, or maybe I'll just sit here until Dad comes in and yells at me.

The doorbell rang. Someone looking for his father, or some service guy calling in to check on the heating system. He opened the door. Ella stood there holding a folder and a six-pack of Bartlett's root beer. "I finally found the root beer at a deli in the East Village, and these are notes for the English exam," she said, pushing past him into the living room. "I went to a special review class on tomorrow's test, and I spent last night studying for it, which means I'm barely functioning."

Sam stared at her. "Last night?" was all he managed to say.

She cocked her head at him and looked, what—exasperated? "Yeah, last night. My parents were going out and my sisters both had friends over, which meant I was the 'adult' in the house. But at least I got paid. And you got this six-pack…. Sometimes, Sam, you're just so dumb. That's all I'm saying. But let me know when you figure it out."

Chapter 19

Welcoming the Bees

Drops of sweat gathered on Sam's forehead, threatening to roll off onto the small hive boxes sitting on The Meadows' roof. *There are living things in there,* he thought, *and they're waiting for us to open the doors and set them free. Or at least move them into their new homes.*

He heard The Bee Team climbing the ladder. Ella, the first to appear, came over and looked at the nucs. "No problem with the delivery?"

That was the easy part. The beekeeper from Basking Ridge had dropped off four wooden bee boxes that afternoon in Bella Vista's kitchen, collected his cannoli, mocha cake and tarts, shook hands with Sam and Nick, and left to attend a seminar in midtown. Nick helped Sam carry the boxes to the roof. "This is your big moment," he told him before rushing back to the kitchen. "May the buzz be with you."

Sam pointed to the hats, veils, coveralls, and gloves delivered to Bella Vista the day before. The team suited up and stood quietly, reverently, before the boxes. "This is amazing," Tristan said, almost in a whisper. "We are about to become home to 80,000 bees who will fly out and pollinate thousands of plants just the way they've been doing almost since the beginning of time. We will witness the life's work of one of the most sophisticated social and communication systems that nature has devised to sustain living things on this earth. It's incredible. We're actually going to be real beekeepers."

The rest of The Bee Team stared at Tristan. Matt finally broke the silence. "Yeah, it's amazing. Are you done with the Gettysburg Address? Can we get on with the bees? What do we do first?"

Tristan pulled out a notebook. "Are the hives facing south? Yes. Did the bricks we got raise them high enough off the ground? Yes. Do we have the water feeders for them? Yes. Are we terrified? Yes. Okay, guys, let's begin."

Sam opened the first nuc box and saw five frames partially filled with honeycomb plus worker bees, brood, and pollen. The queen had been laying eggs there for about a month, according to the New Jersey beekeeper, and the frames had filled out just enough to be moved into the permanent hive.

He picked up a frame from the nuc and dropped it into a deep in the nearest large hive, then moved the other four alongside it, replacing five of the frames that were already there. The process was repeated three times.

After a few minutes, the four beekeepers heard the bees moving around their new homes, a light scratching noise like the gentle crumpling of tissue paper. Some of the bees ventured out, took a few spins in the air and then returned to the entrance. "Like I said, amazing," whispered Tristan.

By the time each hive had its bees and queen, plus food and water, it was dusk. The new beekeepers sat silently a few feet away from the four slightly tilted, homemade, bizarre-looking, beautiful structures. It was one of those moments when Sam could believe things were working out, that maybe their project would be a success, that Bella Vista would be number one again, that he and Nick could stay in Manhattan.

I'm like the bees, he thought. I was packaged up and brought to a whole new place, gently dumped into a new home and helped in the transition by many people, including the three sitting next to me. Especially those three. He looked at each one and smiled. By now it was too dark to tell, but he was pretty sure each one of them smiled back.

Chapter 20

Moonlight at the Motel

The Bee Team met at Tristan's apartment Friday afternoon carrying four small duffel bags plus five lunch boxes packed by one of Nick's assistants at Bella Vista. Destination: the Pennsylvania Apiary Center in Fairfield, Pa.

Ron, Tristan's dad, was the chauffeur/chaperone, and transportation was his slightly battered Honda CRV parked in a garage two blocks away. Matt immediately claimed the front passenger seat. "I'm bigger than anyone else," he said, quickly adding, "stronger, too."

"You mean fatter, too," said Ella. "But that doesn't earn you any points. Come on, we can all take turns squeezing into the back and living in luxury in the front. Teamwork, Matt? Think of the bees. None, except maybe the drones, would try to claim more space in the hive than the others."

They arrived in Fairfield at seven p.m., ate dinner, and checked into the small town's only motel—one room for Ron, one for the three boys (twin beds plus a cot), and one for Ella. Ron switched from designated driver to parent: "Get to bed. Breakfast is eight thirty sharp, then checkout, and then we meet Paul at nine thirty. I'm told that anyone who keeps a beekeeper waiting is asking to get stung." He winked at them and received sickly smiles in return.

The boys headed for their room, next door to Ella's. Sam watched her as she waved good night. At that exact moment, an idea bloomed in his head that was so dazzling, so brilliant, so daring that he actually felt dizzy. Was he crazy? More importantly, could it work?

Inside the motel room, Matt immediately put his duffel bag on one of the beds. Sam looked at Tristan. "Fine," Sam said. "Your father drove us here. I'll take the cot." He tested it out. It felt like a bunch of screws covered by an exercise mat, and it sagged so much that a part of his back dropped six inches lower than the rest of him. "I'd be better off on the floor. Let's just go to bed." That wouldn't happen for another three hours. Matt watched a late night sci fi movie before finally switching off the wall light. Five minutes later, he was asleep.

Sam, however, was wide awake. It's now or never, and maybe never is the right answer, he told himself. I could get in huge, irreversible, life-ending trouble—with my father, my school, my friends. What am I thinking? I'm thinking I need to be really quiet, he told himself as he rolled gently off the mattress onto the floor, picked up one of the room keys, and let himself out into the covered walkway. Halfway down the corridor he could hear music, but next door was quiet.

He knocked gently, then a little harder. "Ell?" he whispered, and waited.

To his utter amazement, she opened the door. "Sam," she said.

"I'm sorry, Ell, but I couldn't sleep. Matt and Tristan took the beds, and I'm stuck on a cot they probably used in medieval torture chambers. Do you think I could just camp out on your floor? I only need a few hours of sleep ... I want to be at least semi-conscious for the bee visit ... I won't stay for the whole night, maybe just three or four hours, or maybe five..." He could hear himself stuttering. Could he possibly sound any more pathetic?

Ella put her head out the door, looked both ways, and yanked him in. "You can't stay in my room, but you can have all my extra pillows and blankets," she said, starting to collect them off the spare bed.

The room was filled with soft light. Must be from the walkway outside, or maybe it's the moon, Sam thought, glancing out the window and then back at Ella, at her hair cascading down and around the shoulders of her oversized tee shirt. A heart-stopping moment—the way she looked silhouetted against the wall, how much he wanted to reach out and touch her. And then what? I'm a clod, he said to himself.

Ella rolled the bedclothes into a big ball and tossed them at Sam. "Good night," she said, shoving him gently out the door and then giving him a wraparound hug, drawing them together like pieces of a jigsaw puzzle locking into a perfect fit. "Make sure you guys don't oversleep."

Sam slipped back into his room, spread out all the blankets and pillows on the floor, and lay down. It wasn't exactly what he had planned. He wished he'd seen Ella's hug coming, could have held on to her, and the moment, longer. Another time.

At 8:25, the alarm clock blasted off next to his head. He shook his two roommates awake and joined Ella and Ron at breakfast. They headed off to the hives.

Chapter 21

A Tough Lesson Learned

Ron pulled into a parking lot near the Pennsylvania Apiary Center and hustled the team to their rendezvous point on the front steps. Tristan walked up to a multi-colored map that hung nearby. "This place is huge, almost fifty acres," he announced. "It looks like a ski resort—lots of trails, a bunch of different gardens. My guess is the hives are placed to maximize the pollination of specific trees and plants."

"You're exactly right." A man in khaki pants and buttoned-up long-sleeved shirt, lugging a duffel bag full of white coveralls, jackets, gloves, and hats, walked up to introduce himself. "I'm Paul Miranda, and I'm going to be your guide." He shook everyone's hand. "The notepads gave it away," he said to Ron. "Most of the people coming here on a Saturday, when we're not hosting school trips, don't bring notepads. But I'm glad to see them. I get the sense your kids are on a serious mission, and bees are serious stuff."

Sam offered a brief explanation of their science project. "Hives on the roof?" Paul asked, raising one eyebrow. "Interesting idea, and you're near Central Park, which means multiple foraging opportunities. I just hope you can keep the hives healthy. Hive infestation is a huge problem everywhere, as I'm sure you know."

Tristan pulled out a small notecard from his jeans pocket. "Can you show us those tiny little mites that attach themselves to the bees and suck out their insides? And the beetles that tunnel into the comb and contaminate the honey?"

"Sure," Paul said. "Unfortunately, I can show you all of that. We're constantly battling to keep parasites, fungi, wax moths, small hive beetles, and other pests from destroying our hives."

Before leaving the Visitors Center, Paul led them around to the back where a man, his face and upper body covered with approximately 12,000 bees, was talking to a group of apiarists from England. Matt gawked. "This guy's crazy! What's he doing? Why isn't he getting stung?"

Paul laughed. "This is a common sight at county fairs and agricultural exhibitions. It's called a 'bee beard.' The man has hidden a queen bee in a tiny cage and is holding it under his chin. The bees are not in attack mode. They are simply doing what bees do: swarming, which in this case means following their queen and landing on whatever they can find to be close to her."

They climbed into Paul's large van. "We're especially proud of our flower gardens, although few of the native plants are blooming this early," he noted, pointing to what would soon be wild geraniums, butterfly weed, and bee balm. "The same for vegetables: squash, beans, asparagus. And trees, including apple, peach and cherry, red cedar, sugar maple, pine, and hemlock. You're seeing us when we're just beginning our annual rebirth. How successful that will be all depends on our girls." He looked in the rear view mirror at Ella. "That's what we call the bees," he said. "I'm sure you know it's a matriarchal society, the ultimate in girl power."

In a clearing with ten especially busy hives, Paul put on one of the protective suits and handed out the other five. "Make sure every inch of skin is covered, especially your necks. The bees won't pay much attention to us because we're not trying to collect their honey, and we'll be staying away from their foraging path," he said. "But better safe than sorry."

"Safe and hot," Matt muttered to Sam, trying to free up the area around his neck. "I feel like I've been stuffed into a toaster."

"Pretend the inside is lined with ice cubes," Tristan said. "Or else imagine what it would be like to get stung by fifty angry bees."

Ella used her phone to take close-ups of the hive entrance. "These bees have yellow and tan bands. But I've seen pictures of other bees that are brownish-grey. What's the difference?"

Paul looked approvingly at Ella. "Great question. It gets to the whole subject of crossbreeding bees to get the best possible hybrid. For example, Russian bees, the darker ones, are hardier because of immunities they developed more than a century ago when they found a home in far eastern Russia and were exposed to the varroa mites. They're the survivor stock. Yet Italian bees are still the gold standard in the U.S. because they're gentler, they're great honey producers, and they tend to swarm only once a year."

The worst, Paul said, are Africanized bees, "which you probably know as 'killer bees.' They're extremely aggressive. They will chase you for a quarter of a mile if they think you're interfering with the hive. But they seem especially resistant not only to varroa mites, but also to other parasites and certain bacteria."

The point is, he added, "when you try to crossbreed, you may end up with bees that are more tranquil and produce more honey, but that also have fewer defenses against mites and disease. Or they may be more productive, but also much more aggressive. You have to experiment with the tradeoffs."

Ella whispered into Sam's ear. "Hey, we could crossbreed Matt with Tristan and get a big, beefy geek that Reed could never beat, at anything. We'd have a bodyguard with brains."

Sam whispered back. "And appetite. He'd probably hit every refrigerator in Manhattan. No cheesecake would be safe."

Tristan looked at his notebook and then at Paul: "You used the word 'swarming' a few minutes ago. What's that?"

"Glad you asked," Paul said. "It happens when about half to two thirds of the colony, including the queen, leave an increasingly crowded hive to find a new home, which could be a hollowed-out tree, the inside of a chimney, or maybe the underside of a porch. What remains in the old hive are soon-to-emerge queens, some brood, young bees and food, all of which allow the colony to rebuild. It's a way for colonies to reproduce themselves."

The group moved on to check out the nearest hive. Even here, in what Paul noted was a relatively healthy one, it was possible to see varroa mites, each no bigger than the head of a pin, lodged in the abdomens of the bees and in brood cells. Further on were signs of small hive beetles, recognizable by their club-shaped antennae. "They sneak into the hives and live with the bees," Paul said. "If the bees are weak and can't control them, the beetles will start to lay eggs. The eggs hatch into larvae, which then tunnel through the hive looking for honey, brood, and pollen to eat. Whatever the larvae excrete from their bodies contaminates the honey so thoroughly that no bee or human would want any part of it. You can end up with a big, stinky mess."

"Do the bees know their bodies have been attacked or their honey has been destroyed?" asked Matt. "Do they have a sense that they're doomed? Is there any way a bee can see these disasters coming?"

"All good questions," Paul said. "I don't know the answers. If bees could talk, I imagine we'd get a lot of very good information."

****

Shortly before the tour was over, Paul opened up one of the hives and pointed to a cluster of bees moving in and around the cells. "I'd like you to see a queen," he said. "Ella, look closely. Anything?"

"There!" she said, pointing to a bee that was about half again as large as all the others. "Her royal highness, the one that makes it all happen."

"Not quite all," said Matt, hands on hips, stomach pulled in—his best macho-man pose. "And where will we be eating lunch?" he asked, already starting to make a sprint for the van.

"Don't walk there!" Paul's voice stopped Matt in his tracks. "Remember? We deliberately avoided the front of the hive when we approached that area. The bees are using that route for their foraging trips. We don't want to block their path. Move away s-l-o-w-l-y."

Uh-oh, thought Sam. I think it's too late. He watched a small squadron of bees begin to buzz around Matt, who launched into panic mode, swatting the air with his arms and jumping around in small circles.

"Matt! Stand perfectly still!" Paul walked slowly over to where Matt was now shaking his head back and forth like a large dog drying itself off. "You're just scaring the bees even more. They need to know that you're harmless, that you're not after their honey. You want to become a statue. Get it?"

Matt didn't get it. "He's going to get stung," Sam said just seconds before Matt let out a series of short, sharp yelps and grabbed at the netting around his neck, alternately slapping it and frantically trying to wrestle it off. Paul was suddenly at his side, pulling him away from the bees' flight path.

Sam huddled closer to Ella and Tristan. "It doesn't take much, does it? A few swats at the bees, and they become as frantic and scared as we are."

They waited for orders from Paul, who had pulled off Matt's hat and netting and was gently probing the skin around his neck and chest. "Everyone back to the van. I need to check those stings right away, although I'm 99 percent sure they'll be normal red welts that will hurt for a few hours and then fade away. That's what typically happens."

Ron sat next to Matt in the middle section of the van. "Take deep breaths, Matt. It's going to be fine. We'll do the baking soda treatment, or whatever they use for bee stings, and we'll stop for a big lunch as soon as we get back on the highway. You'll have a good story to tell once we get home. You've taken one for the team. It can be part of your report. You know: 'How I Survived an Attack by a Horde of Angry Bees.'"

Ella reached over from the back seat to gently pat Matt's shoulders and promise him he could sit in the front seat the whole way back. Tristan was ignoring everyone, making a point of looking out the window. It's how he deals with someone in distress, Sam thought, remembering his visit to Tristan's room. He doesn't know what to say, so he withdraws until he can figure out a way to respond.

The van turned into the Visitors Center parking lot. Matt's neck looked like it had been pumped full of air, and his breathing sounded ragged. "Are you allergic to bee stings?" Paul asked as he helped him out onto the pavement.

"I don't know." Matt looked up. "I've never been stung... I'm feeling dizzy. My mouth feels funny. I need to lie down." He leaned against a concrete pillar.

"Listen, Matt," Paul said. "Here is what's going to happen. I'm calling 911, and we'll get you into an ambulance because the swelling is beginning to spread up to your face. A hospital can treat this, but we need to get you there fast. Understand?"

Matt nodded. Ron put his arms around him, trying to shield him from a small crowd of tourists that had begun to gather on the steps.

"This is bad." Ella took Sam's arm. "Even Paul looks shocked. Someone needs to call Matt's parents. They'll probably want to come out here. Who's going to do that? Maybe we should wait until we know what's going on. I almost feel like it's our fault. I mean Matt was getting restless. We could all see that. Maybe we should have insisted on leaving the hives sooner. Then he wouldn't have been moving so fast. Maybe Ron will call his parents. Maybe Matt will have to spend the night here… We should stay with him, don't you think? I mean that's what friends do. We're a team. Like Ron said, he took one for the team."

She began to cry, little choking sounds punctured by sniffs and hiccups. Sam pulled her into his chest and patted her head, her neck, her ear. "It's okay. It's not anyone's fault. Ron will contact his parents. He's going to be fine. They know what to do about bee allergies." I'm running out of words too, he thought.

Ron rode with Matt in the ambulance, while Paul followed in the van with the rest of the team. Sam's arm remained glued to Ella's shoulders. "What do you think will happen?" he finally asked Paul. "Will Matt be all right?"

Paul nodded his head, saying only that Matt was clearly allergic to bees, and that hospitals are equipped to deal with this situation.

Chapter 22

Parental Intervention

Peeking inside the small, curtained-off corner of the emergency room, Sam could see right away that Matt's cheek, upper lip, chin and neck were puffed up, like his face had been cooked into a giant soufflé. He could also see that Matt was sitting up in the hospital bed drinking a milkshake.

"I think he's going to make it," Sam said. "The milkshake gives it away."

Ron interrupted him. "This is horrible. I should have kept a closer eye on Matt. I feel like this is all my fault. I never—"

Paul cut Ron off. "It's no one's fault, Ron. Matt is one of a very small number of people—around one percent of kids, three percent of adults—who react this way. Normally, people stung by a bee just get localized swelling, not a huge allergic reaction. Matt is one of the unlucky ones."

The good news, Paul added, is that "tests are now available to diagnose insect allergies, and there are treatments to reduce the symptoms. In any case, Matt will get an EpiPen—short for epinephrine, also known as adrenaline—which will immediately reduce his body's allergic response should he ever get stung again. I predict this won't happen now that he knows about his allergy."

Matt suddenly called out to The Bee Team. "Hey guys, come on in. I'm feeling okay, just a little blitzed and my neck hurts. But nothing like it felt when I got stung. That was bad. There must be an easier way to get a milkshake." His face looked even worse when he smiled.

By now, Matt's parents had arrived, and Sam saw them huddled with a doctor a few feet away. He could hear only some of the conversation—"fine after a day or two..." "recommend follow up at home..." Matt's parents nodded, the doctor left, and everyone gathered around Matt's bed.

Matt's dad cleared his throat and looked at Sam. "Listen, Sam. Matt's mother and I do not want Matt continuing on with this bee project. We didn't know he was allergic to stings, but now that we do, we need to keep him as far away from bees as possible. I'm sorry if this poses a problem, but Matt's health is more important than a school assignment. I'm sure you all can see that." He looked at Ella and Tristan.

"Yes, sir," was all Sam could think of to say. That's how you would respond to anything this person suggested, Sam thought. He's physically big, like Matt, he has a loud voice, and he's an executive in a big investment bank, plus he's chairman of the Manhattan School for Science's parents association. He's used to being listened to.

He noticed Ron gearing up to speak, but this time it was Matt who interrupted. "Dad, that's not possible! There's no way I can back out of the project. I have that Epi thing, Epipin, pen, whatever it's called, I can use if I get stung again."

Matt's mother patted his arm. "I know you're disappointed,

Matt. But the answer is no. We'll be able to check you out in half an hour, and we'll be home in time for a late dinner. Right now your father and I are making a quick run to the cafeteria. We got the call from Ron just as we were sitting down to lunch. Besides, this will give you some time with your friends. Ron, would you like to join us?"

Paul left, too, heading back to lead the afternoon hive tour. The Bee Team was finally alone.

"Guys," Matt said. "This is all my fault. I'll get off the team. All I do is mess things up. As usual. Let's face it. You'd be better off without me."

Sam weighed in first. "Matt, I'm not saying we want you off the team, but I kind of get your parents' point. You didn't see yourself in the van on the way here. It was pretty scary."

Ella turned on Sam. "So what are you saying? That we don't need him? That we should just drop him because of one—okay, a few—bee stings?" Her eyes actually flashed. At *him*.

"No!" Sam did a quick U-turn. "No, I'm not saying that. I'm just pointing out that whatever we do, we have to make sure Matt never ever gets stung, even if it means wrapping him up in four layers of protective clothing and covering him with a lead shield."

Tristan spoke quietly. "That assumes that we are all going to ignore Matt's parents. They weren't exactly unclear about their expectations." He paused. "Then again, he can't just drop out of the science competition. What's his alternative? Do a project on his own? Join another team? Maybe we could find him a role that isn't on the front line."

Matt waved his arms. "Hey, guys. I'm still in the room. You're talking like I'm not here. But keep going. You're all smarter than me anyway. You'll figure something out."

Ella looked at him. "I agree with Tristan. There's a solution that we just haven't thought of. But from now on, Matt, stay away from anything that flies or buzzes. You're already behind on the research you're supposed to be doing. You need to step it up."

"What she means," Sam said, lightly pressing Ella's hand and feeling it press his own hand back, "is that we need you. Without you, we're the B minus Team."

Chapter 23

Night on the Roof

The Bee Team's sleeping bags lay strewn around the roof a few feet away from the hives. It was 10:45 p.m., and the science project sleepover was underway. Sam had convinced Nick that the team needed to observe the bees at different times during the night to see if they actually slept, and if so, for how long and where, and did they move around or stay in one section of the hive – all questions on Tristan's laptop waiting for answers. It would be a very small part of their final report, but at least it would be original research.

Tristan called up a file. "11 p.m. Check current activity in hives," he read off. "Okay, guys. Let's take a look. But be quiet. And don't shine flashlights into the hives. That would scare the bees. Matt, remember, you agreed to stay twenty feet back from the action, if there is any."

Matt had also agreed, very reluctantly, to wear his protective bee suit and veiled hat the whole night. Sam suspected he hadn't told his parents about the bee part of the sleepover, but there was no point now in asking. The bee check was about to begin.

The other three Bee Team members pulled on their protective suits. Ella grabbed her sketchpad, and they moved in slowly, a bulked-up SWAT team scouting out what they hoped would be a friendly, rather than hostile, target.

Sam lifted off one of the covers, and they all peered in. Some of the bees were completely still. Others moved slowly around the hive entrances, their tiny bodies barely moving, like little wind-up dolls on their last spin. A group of more alert bees tried, unsuccessfully, to crawl up The Bee Team's arms and legs.

Ella worked on a few drawings, then turned around to look back at Matt. "I'm watching you," she said. "Don't even think about coming close, or leaving off even the smallest piece of that suit. The crowd this time isn't screaming, 'Take it all off,' Matt. They're screaming, 'Keep it all on.'"

Another ten minutes and the first shift of the nighttime bee watch ended. "Not much happening," Tristan said, heading for his sleeping bag. "Our second shift should be around 2 a.m., the likeliest time more bees will be sleeping. And it means we can sleep a little, too. Matt, try not to snore or grind your teeth or make those slurping noises. I'm a light sleeper, and I know you're not."

Sam set the alarm for 2 a.m. He needn't have bothered. There was no way he was actually going to fall asleep. At midnight, he looked over at Ella. She lay on her side, curled up with her back to him, totally still. He stared up at a night sky brilliant with stars until the beep-beep of the alarm signaled time for the next bee check.

Tristan rolled out of his sleeping bag, put on his sweater, and looked over at Ella. He gave her a few gentle shoves until her head popped out of the sleeping bag. "Let's do it," she said, reaching for her sketchpad. "Has someone woken up Matt?"

That proved to be unusually difficult. Matt lay awkwardly on his back, his head barely visible through the veiled hat, his body enveloped by what looked like a deflated parachute. Tristan shook him a few times. Sam shook him a few more times. Matt's snores, muffled by the hat, didn't miss a beat.

"I vote we just let him sleep," said Sam. "I think we can manage the check on our own."

Everything was silent. Tristan quietly lifted off another of the hive covers. "Very little movement, except for a few outliers at the edges of the honeycomb," he said. "There is still some minimal activity going on, but I think we can safely conclude that most of the bees have turned in for the night."

He made a few notes and and closed his laptop. "I'm going back to the living room and sleep on the couch. It's cooler up here than I thought. I'm not sure my flannel-lined, insulated, down-filled sleeping bag made for critically cold, sub-zero conditions will keep me warm enough, so you guys are on your own. Keep a close watch. And yes, I don't think I would bother waking Matt up. He'll sleep until someone waves a chocolate chip muffin in front of his nose."

We will be friends forever, Sam thought, watching Tristan head for the roof ladder. He looked at Ella. "Hey, Ell. Tristan's right. It's pretty cold up here. If you want to move your sleeping bag closer to mine, it would probably help to keep us warm. I'll set the alarm for five, and we can have another look at the hives. I have a note pad …"

He stopped talking as Ella rearranged her sleeping bag just inches away from his own. "Shut up. You'll wake Matt."

They slid under their covers and lay there without moving until Sam slowly reached his hand out to Ella, and they both turned towards each other at exactly the same moment. Ella's face in the moonlight looked fragile, sculpted from ivory. I want time to stand still, Sam thought. I want to always be on this roof, under these stars, next to this person. I want this to last forever.

He moved his sleeping bag so that its edges overlapped the edges of Ella's, and pointed to the hives. "Ell," he whispered. "I think our bees are rubbing off on us. You know all the research Tristan did while he was at home with his broken rib? One thing he told me was that in winter, bees cluster together in a tight ball in the middle of the hive. The bees on the inside of the ball do this 'shivering' motion to generate heat, while the bees on the outside act as insulators to hold the heat in. They take turns being on the inside and outside so all the bees get a chance to be warm."

Ella burst out laughing. "That's kind of what we've done, Sam. We're doing our own insulating and heating, all the things those smart bees do. And they figured this out eons ago."

Do bees fall in love, he wondered. Do they look at the bee they are lying next to and hope they will always be lying next to that same bee? He turned to Ella. "I feel like we're losing our insulation. I think we need to cluster."

Four hours later, Sam heard Tristan rattling the roof door to announce his arrival, emerging seconds later with a bag of muffins provided by Bella Vista's kitchen. Sam and Ella quickly turned their backs on each other and lay against the separate sides of their sleeping bags. Sam spoke loudly: "Time to wake up already?" Tristan was just as loud: "Yes. Time for our last bee check. I'll wake Matt, but before I do, you might want to take a muffin. In approximately two minutes, there won't be any left."

One more hive inspection, a few more photos, and The Bee Team descended back down the ladder. "We can probably get in a couple more hours of sleep on your living room floor," Tristan said. "Our night of strenuous research is over, and I would say, Sam, that it's been very successful. Wouldn't you agree?"

Chapter 24

What Would the Bees Do?

Tristan and Sam walked up the steps to the technology center at Columbia and asked the guard at the front desk where they could find the cafeteria.

"Don't you know?" Sam asked Tristan while they headed off down one of the corridors. "Isn't this where you take your programming course?"

"Yeah, well, I don't come here to eat," Tristan said. "I have barely enough time to make it to class once last period ends. Anyway, I think this is it." He pointed to glass doors leading into a big room with a long food counter and students sitting at tables, mostly alone, staring at their laptops. "Where do we start?"

For once, Sam thought, I don't have a plan. It was only two days ago that Tristan told him he saw Reed and Miles enter the Columbia building just ahead of him and meet up with an older-looking student in an unlit corner of the lobby. Tristan watched Miles give the Columbia student a handful of cash and then a notebook and some folders.

The goal today was, scientifically speaking, to test out their hypothesis that the Robots R Us team was cheating and then draw a conclusion from their findings.

So maybe the best approach was a straightforward one: Ask a couple of the students in the cafeteria if they knew anyone Sam and Tristan could hire to help them with a seventh-grade science project. "That could be pretty awkward," Tristan said. "Go ahead. You take the lead."

Sam walked up to one of the few tables where a conversation was going on among three students who looked like they might be having their first meal of the day—cereal and juice. "Excuse me," he said. "My friend and I are doing a science project for school, and we're looking for some computer help, someone who could write a customized program for us. Do you have any ideas?"

One of the students looked interested. "Yeah, I know a guy in one of my classes, Adam, who's programming for another project at some midtown school. He said it had to do with robots. So, are you willing to pay for this help? What's the project, and how much time would it take?"

Sam zeroed in on the first question. "Do you know how much your friend is getting paid? Then we could decide whether we can move ahead."

It turned out Reed and his team gave the Columbia student $1,000, and the money was paid upfront. "Wow." Sam bit his lip, ran his hand over his head, and hoped he was portraying someone who looked shocked. "That's a lot of money. We're going to have to think about this, check a few things out. But thanks for this information. It's more helpful than you realize."

Back out on the street, Sam erupted into a quick succession of fist pumps. Success! They had tested their hypothesis, and the result, if not absolutely conclusive, was close enough. He looked at Tristan. "So what do we do now?"

******

"This is so bad," Tristan said to Sam the next morning as they met up in the school's courtyard. "I thought last night about all the possible outcomes. On the simplest level, we're in trouble if we report them, and we're in trouble if we don't. I almost wish I'd never seen Reed hand over that money."

He spied Ella and Matt and waved them over. "What's up?" Ella asked. "Your text made me think maybe Reed had snuck into The Meadows and tossed our hives off the roof, or something equally evil."

Sam, looking around to make sure no other students could hear them, presented the facts.

"It sounds like a familiar plot line," Matt said. "One where the rich, spoiled kids do really bad things to win the game, and then they get caught by a gang of superheroes and … what? How does this end?"

They brainstormed. From Sam: Find the guy at Columbia and confront him—hard to do, and why would he admit doing this? From Tristan: Give the problem to Hineline and ask for advice—she would need evidence before she could take any action. From Matt: Lock Reed in a closet and don't let him out until he dictates a confession—an appealing strategy but one that would get The Bee Team in more trouble than Reed. From Ella: Tell the Evil Ones we know what's going on—they would deny it.

"They'll say we're just trying to discredit them," she said. "Since we have no proof—you didn't by any chance record the interaction, did you, Tristan?—that will be a pretty good defense. And we're the ones who'll end up looking bad."

She looked at Sam and Tristan. "Remember, we're not exactly blameless. You guys spied on Reed, and then you lied to someone in order to get second-hand information." She thought for a minute: "So here's a different way to look at it. Ask ourselves: WWBD. What Would the Bees Do?"

Chapter 25

Progress Report

"Do we tell her about the cheating?" Sam turned to his teammates as they huddled outside Ms. Carlisle's door. It was time to deliver a progress report to their advisor.

"Definitely! We tell her!" Matt's voice ricocheted off the walls. "She's been at the school for a million years. She'll know what to do."

Sam wasn't so sure, but at that moment the door to the lab opened, and Ms. Carlisle waved them in.

The Bee Team sat in four chairs arranged in a semicircle around her desk. Sam spoke first, outlining the main points of the project, including the team's visit to the apiary center. Tristan explained how they had ordered and set up the nucs and hives, and done their observation of bees' sleeping habits. Matt described what he had learned about bee stings, and Ella reported on their research into Colony Collapse Disorder. Ms. Carlisle listened without interrupting, occasionally writing notes on a yellow pad pulled from the bottom drawer of her desk.

"Good so far," she said, finally sitting back in her chair like a barge slowly easing into its mooring. "The nighttime study of the bees at sleep shows some initiative, and your report on CCD shows a clear understanding of the conflicting theories about its causes. Yes, all good." She paused.

Here comes the "but," Sam thought. There's always a "but."

"But I will stress again that you must continue to seek out something new or untested—beyond your sleep study—about bee culture, or about CCD, or anything that shows your immersion into your topic. It will suggest that you know where future research should be directed, even if you are not the ones who will be doing that research. So keep digging."

Silence. Tristan looked at Ella. Ella looked at Matt. They all looked at Sam.

Ms. Carlisle's eyes scanned the group. "I sense there is something more to report," she said, folding her hands over her lap. "Sam?"

Sam inhaled, and then in a short, explosive exhale, uttered just one word: "cheating."

"Cheating." Ms. Carlisle repeated it so quietly that Sam almost didn't hear her. "Explain," she said, louder.

Sam and Tristan told her about their trip to Columbia University and their conclusion, admittedly not based on hard scientific evidence, but certainly inferred, that one of the teams was using a college programmer to handle the most difficult part of their project. Ella described the destruction of their materials just before the faculty presentation back in February. Matt jumped up and re-enacted a certain individual's vicious attack on Tristan during spring baseball practice.

Ms. Carlisle rapped out a series of questions: Why hadn't they reported the cheating? Had they tried to confirm it, and what had they done that might get them in trouble? And finally, what were the names of the students who were cheating? Sam hesitated and then told her.

She leaned back in her chair and nodded—not at me, Sam realized, but to herself. "I am not surprised to hear this," she said. "There is an old saying that comes to mind, about children repeating the sins of the fathers. Soon you may understand what that means."

She went on. "I am not going to condemn the action you took against your classmates, provided that, at the right moment, you tell Ms. Hineline what you have done. She will be the one to judge the consequences. It is not for me to say. Nor do I feel a responsibility to pass on this information. The school long ago stopped listening to me. There is no reason it would be any different now."

Sam watched her, trying to puzzle out the emotion behind the words she was so carefully choosing. It's sadness, he finally decided. It's grief for something lost, something that may be gone forever. Whatever happened, it changed her life.

Ms. Carlisle stood up abruptly. The meeting was over. "Good luck. I'm here if you need to talk about anything, anytime."

*****

Out in the hallway, on their way to the stairwell leading to the first floor, Matt stopped and faced his teammates. "Can you believe it? Carlisle's not going to do anything about the cheating. She copped out on us. Some advisor."

Ella nodded. "So much for relying on expertise and experience. It looks like we'll have to handle this ourselves. Ideas, anyone?"

Sam hesitated. "Listen, guys. I get why Carlisle punted on this. She's right. She doesn't have any role in this school anymore. Look at where her office is. Look at the job they gave her. If she tried to help us, it would backfire. We don't have proof of the cheating yet, and she doesn't either. We'd all be seen as troublemakers, and Reed would just keep getting away with it all, as usual. Ella's right. It's up to us."

Chapter 26

Attack of the Hive Beetles

It was Sam and Ella's turn to do the bee check. "We're on a roll," Sam said as they stood waiting for the elevator to take them to the roof. "Dad told me this morning that Armand is paying us $500 for the cleanup. So with the $400 from the bake sale and $200 from the school, we're more than halfway there. We just need about $900 more."

They began to pull frames out of the first two hives, holding them up to the sun to check on the inmates and their honey-making operation. Sam froze. "Ella! I can't believe this! Beetles! Tons of them!" He pointed to small hive beetles scuttling around looking for dark places where they could hide, away from the light and the two shocked beekeepers. Three of the hives had been invaded, but the fourth hive seemed healthy, no intruders in sight.

"I remember Paul, the guy from the apiary center, saying that the eggs of small hive beetles are the biggest problem," Sam said. "When they hatch, the larvae contaminate the honey so badly that no bee or human will go near it."

Signs of that were already visible in the three stricken hives. "This is horrible." Ella was practically wailing. "How did it happen so quickly? Last week everything looked good. Now this is Death Valley."

Not just for the bees, Sam thought. This could sink our whole project, my scholarship, Dad's job, everything. If God is by any chance a bee, now is the time to step up.

He pulled out his cellphone. "Paul gave me his contact information when we were at the hospital. I never thought I'd be calling him," he said as Ella, crouching down next to one of the hives, looked up and flashed him a quick, encouraging smile. This is what they mean by "photo op," Sam thought while waiting for Paul to answer—Ella on the roof, against a blue sky, leaning against our hives, hoping for a miracle, believing it will happen.

"Paul!" Sam said. "Thanks for picking up. We're facing total ruin, and we need your advice." He explained the afternoon's discovery.

Paul let out what sounded like a groan. "I'm not surprised. A lot of beekeepers have reported that the small hive beetles are especially bad this year. Here's what you need to do. Buy small hive beetle traps, the kind that come with vegetable oil already spread along their bottom trays. Place them around the frames. You'll see small slits at the top. When the beetles start getting attacked by the worker bees, they'll try to escape by crawling into the slits. Once inside, they become coated with the oil and drown."

Sam repeated the information to Ella, thanked Paul, and hung up. "Great," he sighed. "More things to buy. Let's just hope the traps don't cost too much."

Ella was way ahead of him. "They don't. I found them online. About $30 each, times three. We'll have to pay more for overnight delivery, but we don't really have a choice."

Ella left to take her youngest sister to softball practice. Back in the living room, Sam ordered the beetle traps. Now that Bee Armageddon is upon me, he thought, it's time to start thinking about Plan B, as in a fallback plan to keep me and Dad in Manhattan, at least for the next six years. And that means finding him a job as head pastry chef at a highly rated New York restaurant.

****

One of the three librarians behind the help desk looked up and nodded her head at Sam. "Can I assist you?" she asked in that universal library-quiet voice that created no sound waves but still managed to be heard.

Sam had prepared for this moment. "Sure, thanks. I'm doing a school project on careers, and part of the assignment involves searching for a job in a profession I might want to enter someday. I was hoping you could show me where the listings are for pastry chefs. And maybe you could also tell me what the process is for applying for a position? I'm not really sure where to start."

That was an understatement. He had chosen the New York Public Library as his resource center and was just realizing how gargantuan it was—ceilings so high you could almost fly a small plane up there, white marble everywhere, tall columns, graceful arches, and huge painted murals. He felt like part of a beautifully mounted, interactive art exhibit.

"An interesting project," the librarian murmured, guiding him to an elevator that took them to a huge research room filled with computers and people. She called up generic "Help Wanted" sections along with the employment pages in trade publications aimed at specific industries.

"Plug the location you want into the search engines and then enter 'pastry chef,'" she continued, her voice dropping even lower.

She also pointed out well-known employment websites—monster. com, indeed.com, LinkedIn.com, and Careerbuilder.com—that post millions of job openings and offer advice on resume writing, networking, and career management.

To apply for a position, she said in response to Sam's next question, "one sends in a resume either by email or by going to a company's site and filling out an application form. Different companies have different procedures, so it's hard to generalize." She patted his shoulder. "That should get you started. I'm here until six if you need more help."

Sam put his head in his hands. This is a stupid idea. It won't work. Why am I wasting my time? I need to study for my Spanish test. There must be another way.

He stared at the computer for a full minute, then entered "New York City," followed by "pastry chef," into one of the job search databases. Within seconds, fifty-nine listings popped up on the screen.

Chapter 27

Reed & Ella's Brief History

Sam looked at Ella as they sat in the school cafeteria with Matt and Tristan. "Are you sure there isn't some past history with you and Reed?" he asked. "Every time he shoots us mean looks, his eyes seem to stay on you longer than anyone. But it's not just dislike; it's something else I can't describe."

Ella folded her arms across her chest and focused her attention out the window. Matt stared intently at Ella. Tristan was absorbed by two classmates at the next table comparing their smart watches.

Okay, Sam thought, so Tristan and Matt both know what I'm talking about. "I'm waiting," he said. Matt spoke first. "Go ahead, Ella, tell Sam, or I will. Consider it part of our motivation for bringing the Evil Ones to justice."

Ella let out a long sigh. "It's just stupid sixth-grade stuff," she said. "Embarrassing more than anything else."

Reed, it turned out, developed a huge crush on Ella last spring. Charlene developed an equally huge crush on Reed. Ella made it clear she disliked both of them, despite repeated attempts by Reed to bully her into joining his group. When that didn't work, he tried to pull her into a closet in the basement on a Friday afternoon when no one was around.

"I don't know what he had in mind, but I pushed him away and started to run down the hallway. He ran after me and tried to grab my sweatshirt but ended up pulling my hair instead. I turned around and yelled at him. Bad move. I think he actually thought I was playing some kind of hard-to-get game. As if! The next thing I knew he had grabbed me by the shoulders, *laughing*, like we were both in on the same joke. I mean who can resist him, right? But I got a break. A janitor came out of a closet down the hall and started to walk towards us. Reed dropped his hands, then started to casually walk away like nothing had happened."

The worst part, she added—even worse than Reed leaving her shoulders with big bruises that would last for days—was what he whispered as he was heading to the staircase: "He said I was pathetic, that I thought I was better than everyone else, better than all the other girls in the class, when really I was just a stupid loser hanging out with all the other stupid losers, meaning of course all my friends. And that I should let him know when I was ready to apologize for yelling at him." Ella shuddered. "Apologize? To him? I would rather put my bare arm in a beehive."

Matt had seen Ella when she stumbled upstairs, hair disheveled, sweatshirt hanging lopsided off one shoulder, her face bright red. "I told her to report him, but Reed has a way of always denying anything anyone says about him. Ella had no proof of what had happened. End of story."

Sam stared at his three teammates. "And that's it? Game over? No one is going to fix this? Reed is dangerous. Someone should stop him, someone should…"

Matt broke in. "Okay, Sam. Tell us something we don't know. Yeah, he's a menace to society. And to Ella. But he's also smart. He knows how to get away with things."

Sam caught his breath. "Sorry, guys. I'm not blaming you. But this is a really bad guy who thinks he can bully people into doing whatever he wants. It's easy to understand, Matt, why you keep talking about good vs. evil and getting revenge. So how about now? I think we're ready to activate 'Operation Payback.'"

Chapter 28

Operation Payback: Part I

Two days later, in the middle of an unusually warm May afternoon, the students at the Manhattan School for Science dragged themselves out of the hot, stuffy computer labs and down to the locker rooms. Sam and Tristan shuffled papers around in their folders, talked about the upcoming history test, and waited for Reed and Miles to make their appearance.

"They're here," Tristan whispered. "Ready to go?" Sam nodded.

He and Tristan pulled out some brightly colored posters from their backpacks and walked over to Reed. "Hey, guys," Tristan said. "You probably know I take a class up at Columbia some afternoons. Yesterday I saw some posters advertising the end-of-semester University Store sale. I read something about robotics on it, and I thought you might be interested."

Sam gave them his most ingratiating smile. "Yeah, I know we're kind of rivals in the science competition, but I think it's okay to share information that's public. And I'm sure you would do the same for us." He thrust a poster in Reed's face and scattered the others on the bench in front of their lockers. "You might want to buy something on the list. No need to thank us."

They watched as Reed picked one up and began to read it. At the top of the list was a book title: "Everything You Ever Wanted to

Know about Robotics." Price: $45, marked down to $29. Under that was an item that read: "How Technology Has Changed the Way We Compete." Price: $32, marked down to $22. The third item showed an array of University sweatshirts: $45, now $33.

But it was the fourth item on the list, starred and highlighted in yellow, that stood out: "Customized Programming Available for Middle School Robotics Projects:" Fee: $1,000, negotiable.

Sam saw Reed suddenly hold the poster up to his face. Five seconds later, he grabbed Miles' arm and yanked him over. The two of them stood there reading and re-reading the text, unaware that they were looking at Ella's handiwork, an original piece of art she had designed and, with help from Tristan, written. Matt and Sam had printed out several copies and glued them on thick cardboard.

Now for the knockout punch.

"Reed. Miles," Sam called out. "Did you see something you liked on the list? It makes me think I should pass those posters around to other kids. Maybe some of them will be interested in checking out the sale."

"No!" The word practically exploded from Reed's mouth. He grabbed up the rest of the posters and stuffed them in his locker. "You don't know anything about our project. And we definitely don't need help from anyone on the F Team. Get lost." But instead of ending with his usual loud expletive, his voice had actually cracked. That was something new. A chink in the Reed armor.

"'Operation Payback' is launched." Sam grinned at Tristan as they left the locker room and headed out to the sidewalk. "Right about now, Reed and Miles are seriously worried. Their first thought: This is just a coincidence. The advertisement has nothing to do with them. But then doubt creeps in. Reed takes the posters from his locker and buries them in the bottom of the trash bin. Sweat begins to trickle down their backs...."

*****

That afternoon, in a booth at their favorite deli one block from school, The Bee Team ordered a round of chocolate milkshakes. "Consider it our celebration snack," Matt said, expertly tearing the paper off his straw with one hand. "This is one of the best days I can remember. Revenge is sweet."

A few minutes later, Tristan gazed up at the ceiling—silent, unblinking, one thumb gently rubbing his scar. He's about to come out with something brilliant, Sam thought, motioning Matt and Ella to keep quiet, don't even breathe.

"This is how I see it," Tristan finally said. "Reed and team might be able to talk themselves out of believing that someone knows about the cheating. So maybe what they need is a more obvious sign that they aren't getting away with it—a loud and clear message they can't ignore, even if they have no idea who's sending it."

Matt rubbed his hands together. "Great! Let's do it. What's 'it'? What are we doing?"

Tristan's eyes gleamed like little copper pennies. "I've thought of something," he said, lowering his voice, "except that it's going to break just about every rule in the book."

Sam looked at Matt and Ella and then back at Tristan. "It's unanimous. We're in."

Chapter 29

Tristan and the 3-D Printer

Ella pirouetted into the Manhattan School for Science's atrium shortly before the bell sounded for class. "I've got great news!" she announced. Her mother was part of a committee running New York's annual convention for architects and designers, a two-day event scheduled to start at the end of the week at the Javits Convention Center on the city's West side.

The meeting drew about three thousand professionals from all over the world, which meant its organizers had spent months hiring a variety of vendors, from food caterers and flower arrangers to office supply companies and floor space consultants. What they needed now was to line up the "runners"—teenagers assigned to deliver last-minute scheduling changes to the organizers, give out directions to participants, hang up coats, charge up wireless devices, and other things no one had thought of yet. The runners couldn't be paid a set hourly wage, but they were eligible for tips by the organizers, who, "as I noted, include my mother," Ella said.

"Wow," said Matt. "This is perfect. We could work every afternoon and evening, right?"

Ella nodded. "Almost right. A lot of people involved in the conference want their kids to be runners, but Mom's sure she can reserve some of the best time slots for us."

****

Three days later, The Bee Team met at 1 p.m. in the middle of the convention's 200,000 square feet of booths and galleries. "Tristan, you must feel like you've been transported to techno heaven," Sam said. "We're surrounded by about a million tech companies. Do you get what they do?" It was nice, Sam thought, to see Tristan actually impressed, to watch him slowly walk up to different exhibits and stand there staring, like a kid seeing snow for the first time.

Ella led the team down one of the aisles to a round table where three adults were talking into pagers and handing out instructions. The Bee Team checked in, pinned on their nametags, and waited.

Five minutes later, Sam sped off to Section D to run messages between the different exhibitors. Tristan stationed himself next to a large map at one of the side entrances to direct food vendors to their delivery points. Matt headed to the cafeteria to help serve food and clean the dining tables. Ella settled into the passenger seat of one of the go-carts used to transport disabled attendees around the Center.

At 4 p.m., they clocked out and gathered in the cafeteria. "Ella," said Sam. "I think the fix was in. Could it possibly be that your mother made sure you were assigned to sit for two hours and be chauffeured around while talking with a bunch of cool designers?"

Ella put on her most wide-eyed, innocent look: "I don't know what you mean, Sam. I was just lucky."

Matt brushed a few crumbs off his shirt. "I got lucky, too. The cafeteria food was pretty good, and people who came in barely ate anything. They sat and drank coffee and talked. I could do this all afternoon."

"Don't count on it," Ella said. "I know they rotate the shifts. An easy one today means you're likely to get a harder one tomorrow." She pointed to one of the aisles that looked especially promising. "Let's check out some of the exhibits. That is, Sam, if you're not too tired."

They spent the next few minutes walking by displays on energy efficiency, the latest in restoration materials, and new office design technology. Tristan stopped in front of a booth he had seen earlier in the day titled, "Nature's Habitats: Saving the Planet." A man and a woman sat in chairs drinking lemonade. An easel covered with drawings and blueprints stood next to a computer and 3-D printer.

To everyone's surprise, Tristan pulled a rough sketch out of his backpack and set it on one of the empty chairs. "I was wondering if you had a minute…"

The man behind the table gave him a quick once-over. "Maybe. Tell me who you are and what you want. And then I'll see if I have a minute."

Tristan pointed to his sketch and explained The Bee Team project, including the need for original research. When he had finished, the man, who introduced himself as Colin and his colleague as Eleanor, suddenly looked more alert. "I don't know much about bees, but I know enough to think that your idea has some potential. Since this is a slow time for exhibitors, why don't we try a few things out on our CAD/CAM system. I'll need more information to get us going."

Without taking his eyes off Colin's huge computer screen, Tristan gave the team a quick take on CAD/CAM. "Computer-aided design/computer-aided manufacturing. It's software that can design structures or products in ways that are faster, simpler, and cheaper than earlier systems. So people like architects and engineers can experiment with more detailed plans and actually see what the final product will look like."

Colin raised one eyebrow. "Impressive. That about sums it up. Are you sure you're not an architect in disguise?"

Tristan hesitated, as if he wasn't sure whether Colin was joking or serious. "The teacher from my computer course at Columbia referred to it once, and I didn't know what it meant," he finally said. "So I read up on it. It sounded pretty amazing."

Colin moved Tristan's chair next to his, and the two of them began to strategize. Within twenty minutes, they had created an image on the screen that intrigued even the two adult exhibitors. "But will it work?" Tristan asked Colin.

"That's for you to find out," he said. "Go ahead and try it." He gave Tristan a five-minute primer on the 3-D printer, and twenty minutes later, The Bee Team was staring at a miniaturized, three-dimensional printout of a very unusual beehive.

Tristan turned to Sam, Matt, and Ella. "I've been experimenting with that new design I told you about a couple of months ago when you came to my apartment. I think it might be something we could present in our report—you know, something original. Believe me, it's original." He saved the software program he had created for the printer and very carefully picked up the plastic hive.

Colin clapped him on the back. "Experimenting is good, and failure is okay, too, if you learn from it," he said, sounding like the author of one of those motivational, get-rich-quick books. "Here's my card. Let me know what happens ... and call me, wherever I am, if you want a job when you graduate from college."

Chapter 30

Top-secret Job Search

Friday afternoon finally came. Just before the bell rang signaling the end of the regular school year, Ms. Hineline posted the names of the eight science competition finalists on a board outside her office. The teams were chosen, a short paragraph indicated, based on end-of-school progress reports plus "other variables" not elaborated on in the brief announcement.

Ella was the first one to the board, just ahead of a crush of seventh graders eager to see both the winners and the losers. "We're in!" She turned and pushed her way out of the crowd, scanning both ends of the hallway for her teammates. She spotted Sam first. "Sam, we're in! We did it!"

Matt and Tristan arrived minutes later, setting up the group hug. They waited for the crowd to disperse, then moved in to check out the competition.

The Microbe Team, the Sports Concussion team and the Robots R Us team made the list. Sam considered those three the ones to beat, and they all, he decided, sounded a lot more sophisticated and game-changing than honeybees.

To make matters worse, it didn't even seem like an end to the school year, given that the six-week summer session would kick off in five days. *Five days.* Sam remembered the vice principal's explanation: Getting classes started almost immediately meant they would conclude by the end of July, leaving students more than a month of real summer vacation.

It's not as if I have any choice, Sam thought. The Manhattan School for Science has a reputation for rigorous academics, including the summer school program. He knew he was lucky to have gotten a scholarship. He also knew how much he wanted to spend the next five years right where he was, at this school, with these friends, with his dad continuing to make award-winning cakes at a high-end restaurant. Why did that seem increasingly unlikely?

****

Later that afternoon, Nick walked into the living room, picked up his overnight bag, and headed for the door. "I'll be home around dinner time tomorrow night," he said to Sam. "You probably won't even realize I'm gone."

Sam scowled at him. "Yeah, sure. Try not to have too good a time. And remember there are two of us in this family. I want a vote in the final decision."

Sam sat and stared at the T.V. screen. Ohio, of all places. Nick had an interview with a huge new restaurant in Cincinnati whose owners were counting on its grand opening to help the city attract press coverage and, more importantly, tourists. All Sam knew was that it was located somewhere in the Midwest, and that it was definitely not a place he wanted to live.

So I can either do my chores or go check on the bees, Sam thought. Easy decision. He pulled out his bee suit and headed for the roof. The only way this day could get better was if the beetle traps were working, and the bees were once again fully engaged in what he so desperately needed them to do—make honey.

Sam moved around the hives, lifted the roof off the top supers and checked out the frames. One of the hives still looked fine; the bee population in the other three looked no worse, maybe even a little better, than two weeks ago. Don't let me down, he whispered to the bees. We're all counting on you, especially me. I'm *really* counting on you.

This is terrific, he thought. I'm talking to a bunch of bees that I'm *pretty* sure aren't listening. And I'm doing what I promised Tristan I wouldn't—anthropomorphizing. He suddenly thought of what his parents went through when he had pneumonia—taking turns sitting next to his bed, reading to him, putting cool washcloths on his forehead, coaxing the medicine into his mouth, listening to every wheezy breath. "If only I had one of those pink antibiotics that would kill all the beetles and their eggs," he whispered into the hives. Okay, really, it's time to stop. You can't hug a bee.

He leaned against the railing that Armand's construction crew had built around the perimeter of the roof—"It's our Matt-proofing," he told Ella the first time they saw it—before heading back downstairs. Tristan and his dad planned to pick him up at six and drive to Brooklyn for dinner at Ron's favorite restaurant.

His phone vibrated. "Sam! Good news!" Ella sounded jubilant.

"Oh, did you find my Dad a job as head pastry chef at a top-rated restaurant in New York?" he asked.

"What? What are you talking about? I can barely hear you." She sounded impatient.

"Never mind, Ella. It was a bad joke. What's up?"

"Money," said Ella. Her mother had just finished a call with the conference organizers and, at Ella's prompting, brought up the subject of tips for all the runners at the event. The number agreed on was $200 for those who worked four shifts, "which of course, included us," Ella said. "Times four, that's $800. So we're just about there! We can pay everyone back, including your dad!"

"Great." Sam knew his voice sounded flat, but he hadn't thought about that particular problem for weeks. There was so much else to worry about. "All we need now is the honey," he said, filling her in on the latest bee check.

Ella stayed upbeat. "We'll do it, Sam. Or rather the bees will do it. They won't let us down."

He hung up the phone and looked around the empty apartment: Too bad you couldn't say the same about humans.

Decision time again: Do chores, or find his dad a job. The job search won out. Sam retrieved the sheets of paper he had printed out earlier that morning: "Twelve Important Things to Remember When Writing Your Resumé." It was daunting—advice about font size, typeface, headers, format, job objective, cover letter, keywords, information to be included, information to be left out, on and on.

One piece of advice hit hard: Be honest.

Strictly speaking, I'm not being dishonest, Sam thought. I won't include any lies. There won't be exaggerations, or false statements, or cover-ups. Okay, yes, I'm writing someone else's resumé, and he doesn't know it. But I think if that person is a family member, and if he and the resumé writer have a common goal, then it shouldn't be a problem. Isn't this what people mean when they say, "The end justifies the means?"

Focus on the plan. Write a resumé and cover letter and submit them online or through email to the employers you identified that day in the library databases. How hard could this be? He already knew his father's basic job history. Much of it had been mentioned in news articles, some of which dated back to six years ago when his parents had opened their suburban restaurant in an old converted gas station. One reviewer had gone so far as to christen Nick "The Cake King."

Just keep it simple, he told himself. Write short descriptions of Nick's last two positions—restaurant owner and head pastry chef. Include key words from examples of chefs' resumés on the web, words like "four-star restaurant," "award winning," "catering," "pastry overseer," "cake designer," "management responsibility." Contact information was a little trickier. He decided to use his own email account since it included only initials and numbers, nothing to suggest this did not belong to the name on the application.

Three hours later, ten employers in the New York City restaurant business had received the resumé and cover letter of a much admired pastry chef looking for a new opportunity to show off his talents.

Chapter 31

The Cincinnati Kid

Cincinnati. Nick was invited back for a second interview, and the company suggested he bring his son along to check out the new city.

Sam barely spoke on their way to the airport. Nick, reading through the online real estate section of a Cincinnati paper and making notations on his calculator, started to show Sam one of the entries, but stopped.

He's probably feeling the invisible fence surrounding my body and telling him to leave me alone, Sam thought.

He stared out the window during the two-hour plane trip and 30-minute ride in their rented car to downtown Cincinnati. After a mostly silent lunch that Nick spent reviewing emails, they began to drive through one of the neighborhoods near the restaurant. "I've got an interview with the restaurant staff at 4 p.m. I can drop you off at a coffee shop before then. Or you can come with me." Nick spoke in short, clipped sentences.

No response.

Nick studied the map from the rental car agency. They were soon driving past a school. "It's a K-12," Nick said. "One of the best in the city, and they have a strong science program in the upper grades. It's a public school," he added, more to himself than to Sam.

A bunch of kids stood scattered around an outdoor area next to the main entrance. They looked like little militias plotting their attack on hostile forces, like newcomers. Sam imagined words in black letters scrawled on their foreheads: "Get Lost." "New Yorkers Not Wanted."

The school buildings must have been designed by the same architects who did bomb shelters—square brown blocks with few windows and plain rectangular doors that seemed intended to keep students, and everyone else, out. I would be the alien, wandering down unfamiliar hallways and dropping my lunch the first day of school, Sam thought. But there would be no Ella to reach out her hand and save me.

They drove around residential neighborhoods filled with small, single-family homes and rows of town houses. A few people were visible on the sidewalks and porches. They could be zombies, Sam thought. The whole place seemed dead, like all the air had been sucked out, leaving a few feeble shrubs and wilted, colorless flowers. No bees here.

"Nice houses," Nick said. "Close to the school, and there's a shopping center three blocks from this corner. Better yet, the restaurant is less than a mile away. Our immediate needs right within walking distance. What do you think?"

Sam turned away from the car window to stare straight ahead. "I think I would like to go to the coffee shop while you go to the restaurant," he said.

Nick paused. "Good decision. Given your rotten mood, I'm better off going alone. We'll find a place for you to sit and be miserable until I pick you up. Our plane leaves at eight. Got it?"

Sam nodded.

I'm sorry, Dad, he whispered so softly that he knew his father couldn't hear it. I'm sorry, but you have to understand. You can say all you want about how it will be exciting to live in a new city, that I'll make friends easily because I am so wonderful, that I will do well in school. All that doesn't mean anything. I love you, Dad. More than anyone in the world. But I won't move to Cincinnati, not even for you. New York is home.

Chapter 32

Caught in the Act

It was the same dream again, the second time this week it had woken him up at 5:30. Even the opening scene was the same: School was out and he was headed to the subway station that would take him back to The Meadows. But the big red M for Metro had disappeared, swallowed up into the concrete sidewalk, and the street corners on either side were no longer named or numbered. People he stopped to ask for help pointed him one way, then another way, and then they, too, disappeared. He was alone and afraid.

He knew he wouldn't be able to get back to sleep. I won't just lie here and feel creeped out, he thought. I need to get up, get out of this bedroom, it doesn't matter where.

He threw on his clothes, grabbed his backpack, and headed down to the kitchen, tiptoeing past his father in a corner meeting with one of his assistants, then out the back door onto the street.

By now, he knew where he was going.

The subway, already crowded with commuters, stopped a block away from school. In another two hours, the building would be clogged with students and teachers, but for now, it loomed up off the street like an impenetrable fortress, except for a few lights from the basement indicating the presence of the early morning cleaning crew. He tried the front door. Locked. Around the corner, a side door was propped open. He slipped in, down a corridor and into the vast labyrinth that was the school's basement.

A left turn, a right turn, two more turns. Nothing looked familiar. And then he found it, the words "Science Lab: B42" scratched into an old nameplate.

The door, when he tried it, wouldn't budge. He turned the handle as hard as he could back and forth and then pushed. The door sprang open, and he practically fell into the room.

It looked the same, even in the early morning. A dull light coming in through the dirty gray window exposed the same assorted collection of insect skeletons, crusty jars filled with bits and pieces of abandoned lab experiments, old microscopes, rusty scales. He ran his fingers over what were most likely the tiny bones of a bird. The touch reassured him, made him feel like his feet were firmly planted on familiar ground, that this wasn't a dream.

In the darkest corner of the room, on an old square-top desk that had been used by students two decades ago, he noted some picture frames leaning against the wall. Two of the photos caught his attention. The first was a young Helen Carlisle surrounded by four students who were holding up plaques and smiling—real smiles, not staged ones. Ms. Carlisle's smile was the biggest of all. Radiant. Two of the students, one on each side, had their arms around her shoulders.

The second frame enclosed a formal-looking citation announcing Ms. Carlisle's appointment to a presidential commission that would offer training to high school science departments in Asian and African countries. The citation was dated 26 years earlier.

And then he heard them—heavy footsteps marching down the hall, stopping right outside the classroom. He whirled around and saw two huge, armed guards whose faces reminded him of those grinning jack-o-lanterns that used to give him nightmares on Halloween. "Who are you, and what are you doing here?" one of them barked at Sam. Before he could answer, the guard grabbed his arms and snapped on a pair of handcuffs. He turned to his partner: "It looks like we got him. Three months of surveillance has finally paid off."

****

I am not a crook. I am not a crook. Sam repeated the phrase to himself as he sat for almost an hour in a small room next to the school's public safety office. I know some U.S. president said that, but I think he actually *was* a crook, he thought, trying to remember who it was and whether he had gone to jail.

One of the guards came in carrying Sam's backpack. He threw it on the table and glared at Sam with a look of distaste. "Okay. So you're a student here. We verified that. And we didn't find anything in your backpack that looked like it was stolen. So what the heck were you doing at six a.m. breaking into a classroom? And you had better come up with a good answer because you're going to have to repeat it to a bunch of people upstairs."

The guard put his hands behind his head and sat back in the chair. By now he just looked bored, like he was babysitting a not particularly interesting kid when he would rather be sending a really bad one to jail. I'm sorry to disappoint you, Sam thought. I seem to be disappointing a number of people. And they are disappointing me. So maybe things are getting even.

Steven Perez, an eleventh grade math teacher known for his shaved head and thick, black glasses, appeared at the door. He looked at the guard. "I'm taking him off your hands," he said, pointing at Sam. "We'll handle this matter internally since nothing seems to have been destroyed or stolen."

A terse nod from the guard. Sam picked up his backpack and left the room.

Next stop: another small room, this one next to the principal's office. The math teacher looked hard at Sam and left, pulling the door closed behind him.

I can almost hear the cell clanking shut, Sam thought. He began to breathe slowly in and out, in and out, focusing on a spot on the wall, trying to relax his tightly clenched shoulders.

The door opened, so quietly that at first Sam didn't look up. When he did, he found himself face to face with the substantial midsection of Helen Carlisle. She sat down, her fortress-like body gently drooping, one layer at a time, like an accordion folding in on itself. She reached across the table to lightly touch his hand.

"Sam, I came in this morning, and one of the guards said someone had been caught breaking into my classroom. Since there isn't much worth stealing, I wondered if maybe there was a very curious student out there—maybe you—who understood that old science projects, even the outdated ones, could be interesting, even reassuring. If nothing else, they are a reminder of the past."

Sam suddenly blurted out the question he and The Bee Team had already asked each other. "What happened? Why are you stuck down there away from all the other teachers? Why don't you have any classes?" For a moment, he thought she wasn't going to answer. Her face froze. He could hear the wall clock ticking. I went too far, he thought. I should apologize and shut up. It's none of my business.

The door opened again, and Sam now faced Matthew Wade,

the Manhattan School for Science's assistant principal. He nodded at Ms. Carlisle, who left the room, shutting the door behind her.

Mr. Wade didn't waste any time. "You have done something very serious, Sam, breaking into a classroom at a time when you thought no one was around to catch you," he said, not bothering to sit down. "Will you explain what you were up to? And then we will talk about the consequences."

How can I explain this to him when I can't even explain it to myself, Sam wondered. But silence wasn't an option. He began with a brief description of his dream, and how he thought he would feel better if he could go somewhere, like a big cluttered science lab, that had things to take his mind off the feeling of being lost in the middle of a concrete maze with no way to get home.

"I never intended to break in," he finally said, knowing how feeble it sounded. "I thought the door would open with a little pushing. I'm sorry for all the trouble I've caused. It won't happen again. I won't do it again." To his horror, he could feel the skin around his nose and eyes begin to get that full, stuffy feeling. Jeez, knock it off. Stay completely still. Think about bees, or a chocolate buttercream cake, or anything that has nothing to do with this moment.

Mr. Wade held up his hand. "Okay, Sam. You can stop there. I know you aren't a troublemaker, and I know this has been a transition year for you, in many ways. Up until this moment, you have navigated that transition remarkably well. I am going to make a note of this in your file, but I think we can both forget it happened and move ahead. From now on, you are not to come to school until the official start of the day. And you are not to push any doors so hard that they 'open' for you. Is that clear?"

Sam said yes, he got it. Mr. Wade shook his hand and headed

for the door. "Good luck with the science project," he said over his shoulder, with just the hint of a smile. "I have three hives in my backyard. I'm very interested in what you find."

Sam leaned back into the chair and closed his eyes, a brief rest before trying to move on from a disastrous, humiliating morning. When he opened them, Ms. Carlisle was there again, sitting in the same chair as before. "You don't need to talk," she said. "I just wanted to make sure you're all right."

Am I all right, he asked himself. And what does "all right" mean? And then, without stopping to consider why he was about to tell this person things that he had trouble discussing with anyone, he began to talk about Bella Vista and his father's endangered job, and the horrible possibility they might have to move out of Manhattan.

From there it was only natural that he told her about his mother and his old school and the things he had left behind when he moved into The Meadows, and how all that seemed so long ago because he had found new friends and he was excited about his science project, and then it was how much he liked bees and how much his team needed to win the competition so his father could keep his job and he could keep his scholarship, and how that was being jeopardized by the Robots R Us team's cheating, and how he and The Bee Team had done stuff that maybe could get them in trouble but that was necessary to prevent the cheaters from getting away with it and ruining his life.

Ms. Carlisle sat quietly through it all. When Sam finally stopped talking, she pointed to his backpack and stood up. "I would like to continue this conversation, but you have a class and I have a student coming to my office in five minutes. I need to be there on time. She is what I call 'biology-challenged.'"

They smiled at each other and walked side by side down

the hall until Ms. Carlisle veered off towards a staircase that led to the basement. "I'm finally going to start cleaning up, getting rid of things I know I will never again need," she said. "Perhaps if you have some time over the next few weeks, you will come down and help me. There is virtue in clearing out the past, as painful as it can be."

She opened the door to the stairway. "I stashed away stuff in old cardboard boxes that will probably fall apart when I try to move them. But decay is part of science, right? Sometimes it's even the most interesting part."

And then, to Sam's surprise, she laughed. Now that was a sound—a warm, friendly rumbling, a cross between a contented cow and a lawn mower. He suddenly felt better, lighter, like he had aced a dreaded final exam and would never have to take that test again. He nodded at Ms. Carlisle and raced off to the main atrium. The official day was about to start.

Chapter 33

Let Them Eat Cake

"We're halfway there," Nick said, eyeing all the ingredients laid out along several counters. "Now for the icing and the decorations. You're sure you're happy with your decision? I mean, you did change your mind about twenty times this past week." He patted his son's shoulder. "I know it's tricky. You don't want to say too much, but you don't want to miss the opportunity to say something important. Remember, it's just a cake. It's not a marriage proposal."

Sam felt himself turning red. "Dad, can we not talk about this anymore? I'm fine with how it looks. I just hope she likes it."

Sam stood over the counter in Bella Vista's kitchen early Sunday morning, looking down at the molds Nick had just pulled out of the oven. Puffing up from the sides of the pans were sections of a golden yellow cake in odd sizes and shapes.

It was Ella's birthday, but Sam only knew that because her mother called Nick and told him she and her husband were going to be away for the weekend, not returning until Sunday night—too late to celebrate. The family would do that on Monday, but in the meantime, could Nick and Sam invite Ella over for dinner, maybe surprising her with a cupcake and candle?

No problem, Nick said, and what was her favorite flavor?

It was almost 2:30. Sam laid out the picture of the house he had sketched on a piece of cardboard, checking off the different cake sections that had just finished cooling. Nick shook them out of their pans and arranged them on a huge platter.

Next up was chocolate icing. Sam whipped together unsweetened cocoa, confectioner's sugar, milk, vanilla extract, and espresso powder, a recipe he knew by heart. "Mom used to tell me I made this better than the chefs at the restaurant." He looked at his father. "She said it was because I loved chocolate so much that it was like adding another very special ingredient to the mix. Mom was always saying things like that. I think it's how she got me to clean the hamster cage and probably take out the garbage."

Nick dipped his finger in the bowl and licked it. "You haven't lost your touch," he said. "Who knows, maybe we can open a dessert shop in Manhattan that sells icing in just three flavors: chocolate, chocolate, and chocolate."

Sam caught his breath. "Dad! What a great idea! We could sell icings and cakes and maybe have a few tables and chairs, and an ice cream bar and a soda machine. I could help on weekends and afternoons, and get all my friends to come…"

Nick came over to Sam's side of the table and held up his hand. "Sam. Stop. You know I was kidding. That just isn't possible, at least not now. I already told you I'm interviewing for other jobs besides the one in Cincinnati. I'll be in Atlantic City next week, just for a day, and Baltimore the week after. I've heard it's an up-and-coming city, with more and more families moving in and good schools."

He paused. "The economy is still soft, Sam, which means a lot of places are either cutting back or not hiring. You know the phrase 'Let them eat cake?' It doesn't really work when people aren't going out to eat as much as they used to." He went back to his side of the counter. "Come on. We need to get out the food dyes and color a few bowls of icing. One final check of the blueprints and we can start construction."

****

A half hour later, they stood back to look at their work. On the platter lay a spectacular cake in the shape of a Frank Lloyd Wright house, the tan chocolate icing emphasizing its long sloping roof, overhanging eaves, low rectangular windows and multiple terraces. On the double-door entrance was a very un-Wright-like decorative detail that Sam finally decided was the right touch: a heart in red icing with the words "Happy Birthday, Ella" in cursive lettering.

Tristan and Matt showed up at 3 p.m. carrying two half-gallons of chocolate milk and a big "Happy Birthday" sign to hang from the ceiling. "Whoa, awesome!" Matt said, looking at the cake. "We should take a bunch of pictures before we dig in. We *are* going to eat it, right?"

Tristan squinted at the terraces. "Great detail," he said, pointing to the miniature plants dotting the terraces in dabs of colored icings. "All we need is a little Ella peeking out of one of the windows."

As if on cue, a knock sounded at the kitchen door. Nick waved goodbye and disappeared into the elevator. Sam lined up Matt and Tristan in front of the cake. "Hey guys," Ella said, walking in with the algebra study notes Sam asked her to bring over. "What's up? Matt looks like he's swallowed a plate of marshmallow cookies."

Sam counted down. "Five, four, three, two, one ..." Three

boys yelled out, "Surprise! Happy Birthday!" and moved away to reveal the cake. Ella stared.

"She's speechless," Matt crowed. "How rare. I should record this moment of silence."

Ella looked at each member of the group. "This is unbelievable. A Frank Lloyd Wright house. How perfect! Who did this? How? I have to take a picture." She started to fumble for her phone but stopped, walked over to Sam and threw her arms around him. Then around Matt, then Tristan. Then Sam again. "How did you know it was my birthday?" She paused. "Oh, probably my parents. They're away, but they obviously arranged to offload the occasion onto you guys. This is so much better."

She snapped some photos just before Sam stuck a big candle into the center of the cake, lit the wick, and signaled to Ella to make her wish. She glanced at Sam, closed her eyes, and blew.

Conversation stopped while everyone ate. Tristan, waiting until Matt had finished his third helping, handed him his backpack. "It's time for us to do a bee check. Sam and Ella, the beetle traps you got are working. The bees aren't dragging around as much, and there's more of them working the hive. We should keep the traps there a few more weeks. Happy birthday, Ella! I'm going to leave straight from the roof and get started on my homework." Matt followed him, carrying off the chocolate terraces.

Ella and Sam sat next to each other on two stools, surveying the platter's demolition site. "I know it was your idea, Sam," Ella said. "You can't imagine how wonderful I feel. This birthday is so different. You're the difference. I'm going to keep you around for all my birthdays."

If only, Sam thought. So maybe this is the moment to fill her in on the rest of the story—why he felt like he was hanging onto a limb that any minute could break off and crash to the ground. "Ella," he said. "I'm going to tell you something that you can't tell anyone else ... and anyway, I'm hoping that soon it won't matter."

Ella gave an exaggerated sigh. "If you don't know by now that you can trust me, then I would have to say you're hopeless. After all, the two of us are sitting in front of our dream house. Or what's left of it."

Sam shot her a grateful look. "Okay, here goes. You know about my mom, and how my parents' restaurant closed a few months after her death, and how Dad and I left everything behind so he could take this job at Bella Vista. But you don't know why their restaurant had to shut down. Dad said it died of a broken heart"—and the other two broken hearts? Why did we never talk about *them?*—"but what really happened is that the restaurant didn't just shut down. It went bankrupt. I figured it out after overhearing some of Dad's phone conversations."

Sam offered his quick take on bankruptcy. "It means you owe more money than you have, you have to sell off everything that will bring in cash for the people who lent you the money, and you have to lay off a lot of workers, including people who have become your friends. So if my Dad worked in one restaurant that went bankrupt, and another that might close because of competition down the street, it would probably be hard for him to get another position in New York as a head pastry chef—at least not one he'd want. He would have to move to some small town a thousand miles away."

He had seen a letter of reference on Nick's bureau written by Simon. It wasn't addressed to anyone specific. It was just lying there—a neatly typed ticking time bomb—so it could be sent out quickly when a job opportunity came up. And even worse than that was the group of men he had noticed in the hotel one afternoon surveying the ground floor. He didn't have to ask. They were obviously there at Armand's request to scout out other uses for the space that Bella Vista now occupied. "It's like they were measuring the size of the coffin even before they have a dead body."

Ella put her hand on Sam's arm. "Sam, don't worry. I just don't believe you'll have to move. You're stuck here with us, with me, for the next five years at least." She leaned in and took his hand, moving her face within inches of his own. "I have this very strong feeling that things are going to work out. For everyone."

He turned to face her just as the back door opened and Miguel and two other members of the Sunday dinner crew walked in. Sam jumped up and cleared off the dishes. Ella offered everyone a piece of cake.

Beaming, Miguel sat on the stool Sam had just vacated and presented Ella with a gift—a six-inch replica of a beehive he had made out of popsicle sticks, toothpicks and Q-tips, all glued together with frosting. A tiny sign on the front read: "Queen Bee."

When Ella lifted off the top of the hive, she discovered a small box of individually crafted chocolate bees. "Miguel, this is unbelievable. You are a genius. You are amazing. You are the absolute best!" She kissed his cheek and gave him a quick hug. Okay, Sam thought. Enough is enough. We're not looking at season's tickets to the Rangers.

"No, I'm not a genius," Miguel said. "Just a builder. I love making hives. I love everything about them. They remind me that all the huge houses and elaborate skyscrapers we put up are no better than these simple structures that are shelter and work space and family space, all rolled into one." He smiled, joined with his colleagues to sing "Happy Birthday" in Spanish, and moved off to start the prep work for dinner.

The party was over. "I'm giving you what's left of Frank's house to take home, except for a piece for Dad," Sam said to Ella, pulling out big sheets of aluminum foil. "You can have it at tomorrow night's celebration."

She threw her arms around him, burrowing her head into his neck, breathing softly into his ear. If I could just push the pause button, Sam said to himself, because this is a magical moment, and I don't think magic happens all that often.

Ella stepped back and gathered up her books, the cake, and the hive. "This is the celebration that mattered," she said. "Tomorrow night will just be dinner."

Chapter 34

Liquid Gold

The Bee Team stood nervously on the roof, unsure where to start or what to expect. We look like astronauts about to start their exploration of the moon, Sam thought, or a team of heart surgeons about to do a transplant, or extremely nervous teenagers suited up to collect honey from hives on the roof of a Manhattan hotel.

Step One: Sedate the bees. Ella, the team's self-educated smoker expert, crumpled a few newspapers and set them on fire in the bottom of the burner. On top of those, she placed pine needles she had collected from an arboretum in Central Park and watched as flames from the newspapers lit them up. She puffed the bellows to circulate the air.

"Probably the most important thing I learned," she said after a few minutes, "is that it's the smoke, and not the heat, that calms the bees. So I'm letting this cool a little before we start. Also, it works better with just a few small puffs. Otherwise it can make the honey smell, and even taste, like smoke. Not what we're going for."

She turned to Matt. "And you are definitely in the backfield. Triple check that your suit, hat, and gloves are on correctly, that you have your EpiPen handy, and that you're as close to the edge of the roof as you can be without falling off."

Matt patted his chest. "I'm wearing a five-piece protective straitjacket that no bee armed with a machine gun, Taser, and bow and arrow could possibly penetrate. Worry about the bees, not me."

Ella advanced slowly on the first hive, removed the covers, and gently pumped in a tiny cloud of smoke.

Step two: Wearing his thick protective gloves, Sam picked up the hive tool and began to pry out one of the ten frames, using a large brush from the kitchen to gently sweep off the bees clinging to its sides.

He quickly moved to the extractor, which he and Tristan had set up in a small equipment shed as far away from the bees as possible. Using a fork, he scraped the caps off the sealed honeycomb and then loaded the frame into the machine's spherical center. He waited as Ella and Tristan repeated the procedure—unsticking one frame from the rack of ten in each of the other three hives and uncapping the comb. The rest of the frames could wait.

Tristan and Ella took turns cranking the handle, the centrifugal force whipped the frames around, and an amber-colored liquid began to coat the machine's walls and then stream down, dripping into a five-gallon bucket through a valve at the bottom. A fine mesh screen filtered out bits of honeycomb and other particles.

They all stared. Sam felt his eyes begin to tear up, and he suspected the others were having the same reaction although the veiled hats made it difficult to tell. This has to be a miracle, he thought. We pulled it off. Our own Gold Rush. He turned and tried to hug Ella and Tristan. Their bulky suits made the effort an extremely awkward one, so they settled instead for jumping up and down and high-fiving through their gloves. With Matt joining in from the far corner, they let out a cheer that Sam felt sure the kitchen staff sixteen floors below could hear.

He took one of the small jars he had brought up to the roof and slipped it directly under the spigot. He filled five more and then let the rest of the liquid continue flowing into the big container. "Six inaugural jars. One for Dad, one for Armand, one for each of us," he said, handing them out.

Everyone, including Matt, took off one of their gloves, briefly, and lifted up the veils on their hats, *very* briefly. They dipped their fingers into the jars, scooped up the liquid, let it swirl around their mouths, and swallowed. Ella opened her eyes, looked at the team, and delivered her review: "Better, sweeter, more delicious than a chocolate shake any day."

The Bee Team had its first harvest—the kickoff to what they now estimated would be a hundred pounds of honey by the end of the summer. Sam filled one last small jar, and when the others weren't looking, put it in his pocket. "It's time to pay a visit to the kitchen," he told the team. "I think we've kept the chefs waiting long enough."

Chapter 35

Operation Payback: Part II

The seventh grade's last computer lab of the summer session started fifteen minutes late due to a higher than usual number of stragglers. But today, there was no reprimand from the instructors. They, like the students, seemed eager to get done with class and get on with their summers. The mood was almost festive.

The Bee Team took seats in the back row, watching as Reed and Miles sat in the middle section, Charlene and Jeremy right behind them. Sam could see their computer screens if he stretched his head around the rows immediately in front. Right now, the screens were blank. Operation Payback, Part Two, was about to change that.

Two minutes later, most of the students were looking at the first set of instructions for the day's assignment. Reed and team, however, had no such instructions. Against bright green backdrops on their monitors, one word in vivid orange crawled across the screens: C H E A T E R S.

They could be part of a synchronized dance routine, Sam thought, watching as the robot team, all at the exact same moment, bolted upright, then hunched their shoulders and leaned forward, staring motionless at their computers. The word continued to scroll for another 30 seconds before disappearing, sunk by the cartoon-like depiction of an exploding bomb.

Reed turned to Miles, then to Charlene and Jeremy. All four craned their necks to scan the back row. They saw Sam, Tristan, Ella, and Matt, heads down, eyes glued to their screens, earnestly reading the first prompt of the instruction set.

When the bell finally rang, four students from two of the middle rows shot out the door as if trying to outrun a swarm of enraged killer bees.

"Wonder what they're telling each other right now," Ella said as The Bee Team walked down the hall. "They can't pretend it's another coincidence. Cheating? They must know that if they're cheating and they're caught, losing the science competition will be the least of their worries." She paused, a sly smile lighting up her face. "I think I'll try and find Charlene, see if she needs any help on that last computer class. It didn't look like she was paying close attention."

Chapter 36

The Plan that Backfired

Nick thundered into the bedroom and stood, feet firmly planted, in front of Sam. "And just what did you think you were doing?" he shouted. "You sent out resumés under my name to places all around New York? To an insurance company on Staten Island looking for an in-house chef? A construction company in Queens that wants a caterer? Restaurants that no one has ever heard of, including one looking for a *short-order* cook? Do you even know what a short-order cook is? And do you know how much this could hurt my reputation? My relationship with Armand? Our future?"

Sam felt as though someone had punched him in the stomach. "Dad, please believe me," he stuttered. "I just wanted to help you find a job, in New York. You're not even looking here. You're not even thinking about *me*, about what *I* want. So I thought I could get things going, identify some places advertising for chefs. I figured you could sort out where you wanted to interview, if I could just get the interviews. How does this hurt your reputation? I was just trying to help..."

Nick's voice dropped a few decibels, but it was no less angry: "I'll tell you, Sam, and listen, because it's a lesson I want you to remember for the rest of your life."

Two of the places receiving Nick's resumé had called The Meadows to inquire why he was leaving Bella Vista. One can imagine Simon's surprise, Nick said, when he heard Nick was applying for other jobs without at least giving the restaurant a heads-up. And one can imagine how upset Simon was to learn that their highly rated pastry chef had applied to be a hamburger flipper in a Lower Manhattan fast-food restaurant.

"So you see, Sam, things that you do have consequences. You can't pull a trick like this and think you can control what happens next. I had to notify these places that, in fact, I'm not looking for a job with them and then explain to Armand and Simon that my son is a rogue elephant on the loose."

Actually, Nick said, he hadn't put it in quite those terms, and his bosses said they understood what had happened, but some damage had been done, and it might continue if more replies to Sam's expertly crafted resumé kept rolling in. "So I suggest you go back online and tell the companies that 'my' resumé is no longer in play. And in the future, you will not interfere with, lie about, or otherwise mismanage my life. Our lives."

Sam nodded. He put his head down on his desk, trying to hide the tears he knew were coming. I just want to disappear, he thought. I want to fall through this floor all the way to the bottom of the earth and never come back up. That's what happens when you drown, right? "I miss Mom so much, Dad," he finally whispered. "I still miss her so much."

Nick stood still for a long moment until at last, Sam felt his father's arms wrap around his shoulders, his hands clasped together against his chest. "I know you still miss her, Sam. I miss her, too. I wish I could bring her back, for both of us. But I can't. And I can't make your pain go away. There is nothing I can do that will change what happened. So I don't talk about it. It's my way. You will have to find your way. I can only tell you how much I love you, and how you have been all the joy in my life for the past year. Please, don't ever doubt that."

He pulled a crumpled paper towel flecked with buttercream icing out of his chef's apron pocket and wiped Sam's face. "Now I've done it." He gave a half-hearted laugh. "I've created my crowning achievement – face frosting. We'll try it out on our guests. That will get their attention, even if our food no longer seems to."

Sam got to his feet. "I'll fix this. Armand won't get any more calls." He turned to look at his father. "But Dad, I belong here. You belong here. That's why I sent out those resumés. For you and me. For us."

****

Today isn't going well, Sam thought after his father went down to the kitchen, so I might as well write the rest of it off. I'll do another bee check and see how much more destruction I've been responsible for.

He climbed the roof ladder and walked carefully around the four hives. The three that had been hit by the beetles were doing even better than before. As for the fourth hive, there was still no sign of beetles or slimy goo. It was a busy honey factory.

He looked more closely at the healthy hive. A white substance was leaking out from the corners, barely visible around the joints that Matt and Ella hammered together during that forgettable Saturday afternoon. It was the last hive to be assembled, distinguished from the others by a slight crack in its entrance ledge.

He came to an abrupt halt and stared at the hive. It was different for another reason, he remembered. The team had run out of the glue that came with the frames by the time they got to this one, and Matt had been forced to use Sam's homemade glop instead. Was there something about his old glue that kept out the small hive beetles? Maybe some part of its composition that the invaders were allergic to, or didn't like the smell of, or somehow knew was toxic? Sam forced himself to chuckle: Nah, How dumb is that. My glue? C'mon. What a crazy idea.

How crazy? And how could he find out? Sam's feet barely touched the roof ladder as he flew down the steps and ran into his apartment. Maybe the day wasn't a total disaster after all.

Chapter 37

Dinner Is Served

Manhattan in late summer: hot, muggy, smoggy, clogged with tourists. Many residents, if they could afford it, abandoned their city for several weeks in August, which this particular year also happened to be a slow month for nectar flow. Sam and Nick spent 12 days with Nick's parents in Charlottesville, Va., leaving the bees to continue storing their honey and repairing their hives. Matt and his family went to their Long Island summer house. Ella's family rented their usual place at the Jersey shore. Tristan, after a trip to New England with his father, took an intensive, two-week computer class at Columbia.

Now everyone was back, and things were heating up—not just for the beekeepers and their honey harvesting, but for The Meadows as well. Nick told Sam that Armand had called in all the favors he was owed. Elaine and Simon did the same. Two restaurant critics and one business reporter were dining at the hotel with the expectation that they would discover something surprising and new at Bella Vista, something worth writing about.

In Bella Vista's kitchen, one hundred small, honey-filled jars adorned with a new gold/black logo and the words, "Honey from The Meadows," sat on top of one of the long worktables. On a tray next to the jars, images of bees printed on cellophane wrappers decorated bouquets of honey lollipops.

If Elaine hadn't kept drumming her fingers on the kitchen counters and repeatedly buttoning, then unbuttoning, her silk blazer, Sam wouldn't have known how nervous she was. He watched her check and re-check the reservation list every three minutes, as if she couldn't believe the evening was fully booked. Apparently the ad she and Armand placed in several newspapers—announcing the kickoff of Bella Vista's new "honey-infused evening, beginning with the first course and extending into your home"—had worked. Word-of-mouth spread, bringing with it some of that elusive buzz.

Nick and Simon's nervousness showed up in an uncharacteristic way: near silence. Normally their voices would be at full throttle, rippling up and down the counters as the kitchen staff began the many steps that would eventually produce a four-star meal for a sold-out crowd. Tonight, the rumble was quieter, but no less intense.

Just before the first guests were due, Simon put the finishing touches on the pre-appetizers that would greet them as they sat down—one honey-coated shrimp on kale with roasted cashews and orange zest. The individual menus, designed to look more modern and show off the new logo, were already in place at each setting.

Nick and Simon moved to stand side by side in front of the swinging doors that led to the dining room. Everyone in the kitchen—sous chefs, assistant chefs, waiters, dish washers, busboys and one teenager—came to a full stop. Simon turned and shook Nick's hand, extended his arms to the whole staff and announced: "Dinner is served."

Over the next two weeks, Simon repeated that phrase to a growing number of diners who read the positive reviews from Manhattan's restaurant critics and wanted to try out the new menu for themselves. Food bloggers joined the chorus. Bella Vista was back in the game.

Chapter 38

Judgment Day

September 10: Judgment Day.

At least three hundred people crammed into the big auditorium at the Manhattan School for Science—students, parents, teachers, a few members of the press and finally, eight teams of seventh graders looking like young gladiators who have just realized they are the Coliseum's afternoon entertainment.

"Are we ready?" Matt glanced at the giant wall clock at the back of the room. "It's almost one p.m. The presentations start in ten minutes. I heard that the judges will announce the winners by four thirty p.m. I'm going to start practicing my waggle dance." Sam, Ella, and Tristan were busy eyeing the competition.

Exhibits, arranged in a semicircle at the front of the auditorium, were each assigned a number.

Exhibit number one: an investigation into impact forces on young athletes' hockey and football helmets. The team used gel brain molds wrapped with plaster bandages in an attempt to imitate bone material. They worked off 3-D images of skulls, conducted research on bone thickness at different ages, and delved into the mysteries of brain density.

Exhibit number two: microbes. The students' access to the Mt. Sinai microbiology lab was a big plus: Videos showed team members conducting experiments using sophisticated equipment as they analyzed all kinds of microorganisms to determine the effect of heat, oxygen and other variables on their survival. A small table showcased a variety of anti-bacterial soaps and scrubs they had tested—research sure to appeal to germ-minded teachers.

Exhibit number three: an analysis of the emission of methane—a powerful greenhouse gas—by mobile and stationary sources in a nearby local business community. Talk about relevant, Sam thought. The team created a methane gas sensor that they used to measure the amount of methane emitted by individual businesses. Even better, the team's presentation included a series of steps businesses could take to reduce their methane emission.

Exhibit number four investigated the support properties of three different bridges – beam, arch, and suspension. Small replicas of the bridges using different materials and design modifications covered a long table whose top had been decorated to look like a flowing river. Sophisticated diagrams accompanying the text came as no surprise. According to Matt, the father of one of the team members was an engineer.

Exhibit number five looked at the effect of commercial development on water quality. The team visited farms, factories, commercial buildings and recreational facilities located next to rivers in and around Manhattan. They tested the impact of the facilities' waste disposal practices on fish and algae, and produced elaborate diagrams showing different levels of harmful pollutants.

Exhibit number six studied how solar panel installations could be improved to maximize their energy output and overall efficiency. A highlight of the display was the team's own prototype sun-tracking device constructed to ensure that the panels were always oriented to receive maximum exposure to sunlight.

Next to last came The Bee Team: A large table displayed bee paraphernalia, including hive tools, a protective bee suit, a jar labeled "Honey from The Meadows," and a set of bellows. In the center, Tristan's innovative 3-D hive held the place of honor.

Large photos of four beehives on The Meadows' roof were tacked onto partitions along with pictures of the hives before and after their assembly. Reports on pollination, Colony Collapse, and other subjects were interspersed throughout.

Next to the large table, the small box unearthed from the deep recesses of The Meadows sat on a pedestal. A tool chest decorated with bee cutouts pasted on by Ella took up most of the space on a slightly lower, slightly smaller pedestal. The chest would not be opened until the judges appeared for the team's final summation.

And finally, in the back of the exhibit on a card table, a grainy video showed suited-up Bee Team members—three next to the hives and one farther back – in the process of extracting honey. Once a small jar had been filled, all four beekeepers turned at the exact same moment and waved at their audience.

The eighth and final display in the semicircle: the Robots R Us exhibit presided over by four jittery eighth graders bearing little resemblance to the cocky quartet that, until recently, had acted like they were already on the train to Washington, D.C. Reed cornered Miles in one section of the small space, jabbing his finger first at his face and then at the computer in the middle of a table. Charlene flipped furiously through a notebook, barking instructions to Jeremy, who ignored her.

They, too, had colorful, slickly produced photos, illustrations, and reports. Robot prototypes on a table in the center—including robots designed to operate a drone, run up a staircase, and walk a robotic dog—seemed ready for action. "Look at them," Matt whispered to Sam. "If Reed were a grenade, I would say we should all take cover."

The six judges began to make their way around the floor. In one section of the auditorium, Sam noticed his father standing next to Ella's parents, and next to them, Matt's parents and Ron. His first thought: How will Bella Vista get everything done today without Dad there? Then, forget the restaurant—Dad's *here!* Sam experienced a rush of joy so profound that he felt lifted a few inches off the ground, as if such a momentous occasion could trump even the power of gravity.

Each exhibit had fifteen minutes to showcase its report to the judges, who had already spent several hours alone in the auditorium that morning examining in depth the various components of the projects, including videos. By contrast, the afternoon was for the public, and it gave the judges an opportunity to hear from the teams in person and to do one final assessment of the projects.

The first six contenders made their presentations. Exactly 90 minutes later, The Bee Team took its assigned place in the exhibit space. The judges and a huge crowd of people arrayed behind them waited.

Sam set the stage, first turning on the video, then pointing to a small poster board with text and photos from the article in *The New York Times* that first brought the bees to the team's attention. He quickly described the process of buying bees and setting up hives on The Meadows' roof. He noted their research into the honey-making process, including—he was horrified to feel himself blush—their nighttime examination into whether bees ever sleep.

Matt briefly described their visit to the Pennsylvania Apiary

Center. He referred to reports and photographs, ending with a cautionary tale about bee allergies.

Ella pointed to the recipe box, explaining where they found it and how they used it to support the project. Next, she directed the judges' attention to the team's research on colony collapse, including charts illustrating the threat that CCD poses to fruits, vegetables, nuts and other foods as well as to the many native plants that rely on bees for pollination.

A chart showing pesticides used by the agricultural industry to protect its crops warned the audience about the possible dangers that chemicals—along with parasites, fungi, pests, habitat changes, and human beings—present to honeybees. Studies were summarized that explained how fungicides, insecticides, and herbicides together form a mix that can be toxic to bees, possibly interfering with their navigation system in ways that prevent them from finding their way back to the hive after their foraging trips.

To emphasize these dangers and to showcase current research, she noted the creation of a presidential task force aimed at reducing honeybee deaths and restoring millions of acres of land for pollinators.

"As part of our in-depth study of bees and beekeeping," Ella continued, "we would now like to direct your attention to a discovery we made this summer that could significantly improve the health of some bee colonies." She opened the chest and took out its contents: one small plastic container of glue.

Sam stepped forward to continue the explanation. "We realized two months ago, when we were checking on the plague of small hive beetles in three of our hives, that the fourth hive was totally healthy. There were no beetles in or around it, even though we had ordered the bees from the same place, at the same time."

So why did that hive escape the beetle attack? "It was when we saw little white globs of glue sticking out of the corners of the fourth hive that it hit us: Maybe it was that particular glue—the stuff left over from grade school—that made the difference. Maybe it had a toxic element to it, or maybe the fumes drove the beetles away, or maybe it had something to do with the bright white color. We had no idea."

They decided to test their hypothesis. Sam explained how they first tried putting glue on the three other hives to see if it made a difference. "The results were inconclusive because by that time, the traps we installed had done a pretty effective job."

Next, they isolated a few beetles in a small box, placed a teaspoon of glue in one corner, a teaspoon of soda in another, and a teaspoon of apple juice in a third, then waited to see if the beetles were turned off by any of the choices. "They all went for the apple juice," he said. "We can't claim that proves our hypothesis, but it suggests at the very least that beetles are health-conscious." A few audience members laughed.

In their third experiment, Ella put two teaspoons of apple juice in the box, one of them surrounded by a circle of glue. "A lot fewer beetles crossed the glue to get to the apple juice, but again, it wasn't conclusive," Sam said. "A controlled experiment, such as using the homemade glue in some hives and not in others, would be the next step."

With three minutes left, he quickly noted how the team had contacted an entomologist at Pennsylvania State University and a scientist from the USDA Agricultural Research Service. Three weeks later, they heard back from the two women that, based on preliminary tests, it looked like the vinegar in the glue might offer some kind of protection against small hive beetles. "They hope to conduct further experiments this fall and will let us know what they find," Sam said.

Tristan had the last word. He pointed to his 3-D plastic printout of the hive. "Unlike traditional beehives, this one has a design feature that allows beekeepers to remove honey without disturbing the bees." He spoke so softly that the audience stopped their whispering and leaned forward to catch his words.

He explained that the design originated from two Australian beekeepers trying to cut down on disruption during the honey harvesting process. The men used frames that contained plastic honeycomb cells which could be opened—not by pulling them out, but by inserting a tool that split them apart and allowed honey to quietly flow into containers. A clear plastic panel showed the amount of honey being harvested. "The beekeeper can relax. So can the bees," Tristan said. "They're on the other side of the wall refilling the honey cells, unaware of the heist taking place a few inches away."

His modification to the hive was a device to shut off the honey flow in case a beekeeper didn't want to take the honey all at once. "Consider it a work in progress," he said. "I'm sure there will be many more improvements to come."

He paused. When he spoke once again, his voice was louder and stronger, and he looked directly at the audience. "What I have learned over these past few months," he said, "is that honeybees are both sturdy and fragile. And essential. They don't just pollinate fruits, nuts and vegetables. They also pollinate plants that provide food, water, shelter and nesting sites for many other species. If bees disappear, our lives will be less healthy, less diverse, definitely less colorful. Our ecology will become unbalanced in ways we probably don't even know yet. We're in danger of losing something that we can never get back."

He stepped away from the table, just as the bell sounded. Their time was up.

Sam's eyes scanned the audience until they came to rest on a small group of spectators who seemed to be clapping longer and harder than anyone else. The Bee Team's parents had been joined by Miguel, Armand, Elaine, Simon, and even Paul, all the way from the apiary center. Two other people were standing slightly behind the others. Ms. Carlisle was one, beaming, continuing to clap when everyone else had stopped. The person next to her looked familiar, but he couldn't remember from where, and besides, there were more important things to think about.

And finally, from exhibit eight: Robots R Us.

The robots looked fine. The humans looked terrible. Reed, Miles, Charlene, and Jeremy stood arrayed in front of their computers, hovering around the keyboards and frantically punching different keys. Reed, Sam noticed, kept looking out into the audience, at times raising his hand as if to identify himself, as if to summon help from someone out there he desperately needed. Sam followed Reed's gaze. It was directed to a young man towards the back who was standing still except that occasionally he hunched his shoulders up and down and shook his head. Sam knew instantly who he was— the Columbia student who had written the software program that Robots R Us depended on for their presentation.

Sam tapped Tristan. "Turn quietly to your right and look at the guy about three-quarters of the way back." Tristan found the target. He turned back to Sam and nodded. When Sam tried to point him out to Ella, he was gone.

So Tristan was right, Sam thought. Reed had carelessly left his team's software program up on a screen in the computer lab, and Tristan, walking by before Reed stormed back in to shut it down, had recognized RoboLogix, the robotics simulation software he had learned about in his course at Columbia. Students who took the time to figure out the program could build and program their own robots, enabling them to perform a variety of distinct and useful functions. The Robots R Us team obviously had never bothered with that part of their project. It was easier to pay someone else to do it.

Easier, but not smarter. At the moment, the team's elaborately constructed robots—the centerpiece of their project— couldn't be activated.

The judges and the audience waited. "Reed," said Ms. Bowers, the judge who had championed the Robots R Us team during the February presentations. "What's wrong? Fix your program. You're wasting your minutes. Miles? Charlene? Help him out. Jeremy?"

Another person, stepping to the front of the auditorium, spoke in a voice so loud, so authoritative, that everyone's attention was now riveted on her. "You can't fix it because you don't know how it works." It was Ms. Carlisle. Her voice drilled straight into Reed. "You realized your team couldn't win the competition by playing by the rules, so you cheated. You hired someone to write the code for you. You are a disgrace to the school and to your classmates."

Charlene burst into tears, nodding her head up and down. "We didn't mean to. We just wanted to make sure everything worked. We never thought it would ..." She was choking on the words and didn't see Reed, his face broken out into angry red splotches, turn and lift his hand with the apparent intention of clamping it over her mouth. Stephen Cain, one of the judges, quickly ran up to stand next to Charlene. He whispered angrily to Reed just inches from his face, pointing to the robot exhibit, his teammates, the audience, the other judges and finally to the boy himself. Reed, fists clenched, didn't budge, as though by refusing to move, he could somehow outlast the whole ugly spectacle playing out before him.

The audience held its collective breath, hypnotized by the decidedly unscientific demonstration that was now center stage.

Reed blinked first. He took one step back and shoved his hands into his pockets, his long neck suddenly thrust forward and down, as if holding up his head simply took too much effort. It's total surrender, Sam thought. It's Reed's way of acknowledging that he has finally run into a barricade not even he can fight his way through.

Another one of the judges approached The Bee Team and tapped Tristan on the shoulder. "Tristan, I know this is highly irregular, but is there any way you can take a look at this? The team is of course disqualified, and we will deal with the consequences of their actions later, but if we can salvage their demonstration, that would at least reward all of us who came to see it."

Matt turned to Sam: "You got to be kidding! Tristan help them? He'd be going behind enemy lines!"

Sam was smiling. "Do you get the justice in all this?" he said to Matt and Ella. "A faculty member calling on another student— apparently Tristan's programming skills are well known—to fix a competing team's cheating?"

Tristan moved up to the computer, sat in the chair, and ran through a series of diagnostics. "It's complicated," he said quietly, his fingers lightly tapping his scar. "But I think I've been able to read the code for the program written by... well, by whoever the team got to write it." He glanced over at Reed. "Go ahead. Give it a try."

Sam saw Reed look out into the audience again, and this time his gaze was directed to a tall man in a three-piece suit who was furtively drawing his hand across his neck. Reed's father, Sam thought, is sending a message.

The robot team gathered around the center table of their exhibit, like broken-down wagons circling a sputtering bonfire. Reed looked at Tristan. "We don't need your help. We don't need anyone's help." He spat out the words, looking defiantly at the students and judges in front of him. "This has all been a waste of time. We're done here. We're withdrawing from the competition."

In a huge room so silent you could have heard the hum of a single honeybee, the judges moved away.

Chapter 39

A Surprise Guest

At 4:30 p.m., the judges returned to the auditorium and handed a piece of paper to the principal of the Manhattan School for Science. She stepped up to the podium, with the seven remaining teams standing in front of her, their backs to the audience.

Sam barely heard the principal's long introduction, all about the excellence of the entries, the difficulty the judges had singling one out, the uniqueness of this particular year, the opportunity for the winning team to travel to Washington, D.C., and on and on.

She finally stopped. "And now, the moment we have all been waiting for." Pause. "Second runner-up... goes to... the microbiology team!" Their project, the principal said, "added to our knowledge of illness and disease in an increasingly interconnected world where our biggest defense against contagion is research, experimentation, and shared information." The four teammates shook her hand and the judges' hands, and moved off to the side.

"First runner up." The principal paused again, scanned the audience, pretended to consult her note pad, and then: "The concussion team! For its investigation into the nature of concussions and how helmets may be better constructed to lessen the damage that our body-bashing, head-bashing, ultra-competitive sports teams experience during their adolescent years." More handshaking, and the helmet team joined the microbiology team

"And now I will announce the competition winner." The principal flashed her most dazzling smile, looked at the audience, at the remaining teams, at the ceiling, and finally announced: "The Bee Team!"

She began to read off their names, but stopped when applause from the audience drowned out her words. A few minutes later, she started again, announcing each team member's name and moving on to the judges' praise for the project. "The Bee Team studied an insect that many of us know very little about. They illustrated the grave dangers these insects are facing today, and noted the consequences to our planet if we continue to ignore what could be an ecological disaster."

To learn more about bees, the principal continued, "the team went beyond second-hand research and became beekeepers themselves, setting up and tending four hives. In so doing, they taught us all some very interesting lessons about a society that, in many ways, functions better than our own. Congratulations for an outstanding, relevant, and innovative project. You have made your class, your school, and everyone in this room extremely proud."

The applause reverberated again around the walls of the auditorium as groups of people rushed forward to congratulate the teams while others headed for the exits. Sam felt himself engulfed in his father's arms and rocked back and forth. Miguel and Simon had left to start the dinner preparations, but Armand and Elaine were still there, patting Sam on the back and looking a bit smug, as if an investment they had reluctantly made hadn't been such a bad bet after all. The two executives posed for cameras, gave brief interviews to reporters, beamed at everyone they saw, and headed to the limousine waiting outside.

Ella lightly pressed Sam's elbow: "Look," she said. The woman who had stood beside Ms. Carlisle in the back came forward as Tristan was hugging his father, and placed her hand very gently on the back of his neck. Tristan turned, his mother opened up her arms, and he fell into them, his head buried into her chest. She spoke softly into his ear, and they slowly walked away to a corner of the auditorium. Ron just stared after them. Matt's mother went up to Ron, whispered a few words and gently led him back to the exhibit where she pointed out a few of the diagrams she knew Tristan had made.

Ella's parents each took one of her hands and smiled at each other over her head. They came up to Sam and slapped him on the back. They thanked the judges and, with one final hug for Ella, they were out the door. "They can still get a couple of hours of work in," Ella said, watching them leave.

Sam spotted Matt standing next to his father, using his hands to draw an imaginary beehive in the air, explaining in detail how each piece fit and what their functions were. Then, to Sam's surprise, he noticed Matt's father and mother walk over to where Nick stood deep in conversation with Ms. Carlisle. Matt's father spoke for a few moments to The Bee Team's advisor. She nodded and headed off.

Matt walked up. "I think my parents are telling your dad that the science competition pretty much saved my life. I mean not really, but you know, it was great to be part of the team. You guys actually thought I could do it, all those reports and presentations, even though we all knew I wasn't always functioning 'at the highest level,' as Ella would say."

Sam started to protest, but Matt held up his hand and continued talking. "And then it was time to build the hives, and things got even better. I was really good at it, using the tools and figuring out the directions, setting up these cool structures."

Matt looked down and shuffled his feet—a sign, Sam realized, of how hard Matt found it to think of himself as actually successful. In the spring, Matt said, "when I worked in the community service afterschool program, we used twigs, straws, cardboard, paper cups, paper plates, paper clips, masking tape—stuff we found lying around—to create really crazy, fun stuff. That's when I realized how much I liked these little kids, liked working with them on projects that had nothing to do with homework or classwork."

Is it my imagination, Sam asked himself, or does he even *look* taller, straighter, thinner, and has he stopped that little rocking motion that usually suggests he is about to launch into something totally wacky and inappropriate?

"I decided," Matt went on, "that maybe I could teach these kids something—about bees, or how to use woodworking tools—that would give them self-confidence, because I know how hard things can be when you don't have it. So now I'm building hives with them, and we're going to visit some gardens in the city. I can even explain to them how pollination works."

Oh, and by the way, he added, his mother almost fainted when she saw the video of him up on the roof with all those bees. "But she and Dad forgave me. I think. Anyway, winning helped."

Nick had one last comment before heading back to The Meadows. "Tomorrow night, we'll be setting up a small table in a corner of Bella Vista, where our superb kitchen staff will be serving a victory dinner to four beekeepers. Be there at six or we will give the table to one of the many people on our waiting list."

Chapter 40

Updating a Scandal

"This must be how Oscar winners feel when they walk up to the stage to get those trophies," Tristan said. "It's like we're celebrities. People I have never talked to are congratulating me on the win and asking if there's any honey left over."

It was the day after the judging, and The Bee Team was still riding high on the victory. An easel set up in the school's atrium had a big congratulatory sign surrounded by tan and yellow balloons. An administrator had scheduled a meeting for them next week to discuss the specifics of the weekend in Washington.

Sam knew that another meeting was going on as well: He had seen Reed, Miles, Charlene, and Jeremy walking into the principal's office, heads down, shoulders slumped: Life in prison or suspension from the school? I would be okay with them getting five thousand hours of community service, Sam thought, something that would remind them—every time they checked off one of those hours—that they had cheated, not to mention all the evil things they did to other students, that they did to us.

Leaving the cafeteria after lunch, The Bee Team was astonished to see Ms. Carlisle walking down the main hallway of the Manhattan School for Science. Sam could tell she wanted to give him a hug. He was glad she resisted. "I don't think I've seen you up here during regular school hours," he said, trying to sound diplomatic.

"You mean, up from the dungeon?" She looked around and lowered her voice. "I have been resurrected. I'll give you a quick summary but you will probably hear the longer version next week when the principal makes some announcements."

Twenty-four years ago, she said, she had reported two teachers in the school for falsifying standardized test scores. Among the students whose scores were being raised, with their knowledge, was Reed's father. After word of her allegations got out, she was told that the cheating could not be proven and that no action would be taken. The top administrators were only interested in *good* publicity, not the kind that could hurt their standing as one of the city's most prestigious private schools.

The two teachers she reported—Ms. Bowers was one of them; the other one moved away—"told everyone that I was the one who cheated. There was nothing I could do to prove them wrong, and people eventually believed it. Rumors, once they're repeated often enough—and believe me, a few people made sure these rumors were repeated often enough—get lives of their own. I wasn't exactly fired, but my days as one of the most popular members of the science faculty were over. If I could have found another job, I would have. But it was a very difficult time to be looking."

Matt's father was a senior at the school—a year ahead of Reed's father—when all this happened, "and he graduated without ever knowing anything about it. He had no idea there had been a problem until he listened to Matt's account of your visit to my classroom. He also told me my science labs were the best part, academically speaking, of his senior year. A few months ago, he began investigating how I ended up being exiled to the basement. And then he decided to do something."

He talked with a few teachers and administrators who had been at the Manhattan School for Science at that time, and he tracked down the other teacher Ms. Carlisle knew was guilty. The teacher admitted that he and Ms. Bowers colluded to change the scores of certain students. He hinted, but didn't say outright, that the students' parents actually paid the teachers to cheat. He also said he felt so guilty that he left the school a year later and moved to another town. "He even gave up teaching. Matt's father reported all this to the administration, and one result is already evident: I will be moving into a new classroom just down the hall." In fact, she added, it was Ms. Bowers' office, "but that's a secret for now. I trust you will not tell anyone."

Sam pulled a small paper bag out of his backpack. "Here. This is jar number seven from our first batch of honey." He hesitated. "I'll probably be seeing you in your classroom one of these days. And yeah, anytime you want more honey, just ask. We have a pretty reliable source that's just an elevator ride away."

He thought he saw tears in Ms. Carlisle's eyes as she patted his hand, but maybe it was just the way the sun slanted in through the skylight. "You had all better get to class," she said to the team. "I've probably made you late, but I think each of you has earned a little slack this week. I've already heard two teachers say they're going to look into becoming beekeepers. They talked about it like they were deciding to buy a few goldfish. I don't think they know what they're getting in for."

Chapter 41

Swimming in Honey

Is there such a thing as too much honey?

The Bee Team's victory dinner was swimming in it: roasted peanut soup with honey-whipped cream, honey-roasted cherry tomatoes, honey-roasted pear salad with thyme dressing, honey rosemary biscuits, and a few other dishes that the four friends would have had trouble describing.

"We're trying out some of these new recipes on your sophisticated palates," Nick said as a waiter laid down a basket of hush puppies with curried honey-mustard sauce and a platter of honey-roasted chicken breasts.

"Finally, something I recognize," Matt whispered to Sam, pointing to the chicken.

What was better than the food, Sam thought, was how crowded the restaurant looked. All the tables were full, each one with individual honey jars and lollipops at the place settings.

The final touch: Nick, followed by Armand, Elaine, and Simon, came out of the kitchen carrying a large round platter with a cake in the shape of ... what else, a honeybee. Its antennae were tiny chocolate swirls, its wings spun sugar, its body covered with yellow and tan frosting. On its head, next to very small chocolate chip eyes, was written a gold number one. Nick gave Matt a cake knife. "It's your duty as a member of The Bee Team."

As Matt gleefully sunk the knife into the bee's stinger, Nick turned to Miguel. "I would like to make an announcement," Nick said. "Since our four science competition winners will no doubt be extremely busy the rest of this semester, and for that matter, the rest of their lives, Miguel has offered to take over the care and feeding of the hives."

Miguel, with the help of two other assistant chefs, would be responsible for making sure the hives continued to produce honey for Bella Vista's kitchen. "He's the natural choice," Nick said. "He has inherited exceptional beekeeping skills from his father. You could say that bees are in his DNA."

Sam—recognizing a knight in shining armor when he saw him, including one with angel wing tattoos—jumped up and gave Miguel a hug.

"But you don't get a free pass, my friend," Miguel said, holding Sam out at arms' length. "Hives need attention year round, not just in the summer. I'll be giving the bees sugar water and pollen patties in the late fall and winter so they stay healthy enough to keep their queen warm and cozy. I'll watch out for wind and water damage, and in the spring, I'll check to see that the queen continues to lay those all-important eggs." He looked at Ella, Matt, and Tristan: "I'll expect all of you up on the roof now and then to help the next generation of Meadows pollinators lift off."

Nick had one last piece of news. The restaurant and other venues had sold enough of the individually decorated recipe cards—priced at $2.50 each—to support the rooftop hives, at least in the coming year, and to pay off any remaining loan to The Bee Team. "You're out of debt ... until college," he said.

The two pastry chefs took bows, just as another dessert waiter summoned the four diners into the kitchen, where the whole kitchen staff had quickly gathered around Armand. He was holding up an article with *The New York Times* logo across its top. "A friend of mine who's an editor there told me they just posted this on their website, and it will be in the print edition in the morning," Armand said. "I have a feeling we're going to have a very busy autumn."

The article, written by a feature writer who was present at the judging, noted "an unusual synergy going on at The Meadows. The winners of the Manhattan School for Science's seventh grade science competition became rooftop beekeepers at the hotel as part of their comprehensive study of honeybees and Colony Collapse Disorder. The honey they collected was donated to the hotel's four-star Bella Vista restaurant whose head pastry chef happens to be the father of one of the winners."

How circular life is, Sam thought. Nine months ago I saw an article in the *Times* about colony collapse, and today, the *Times* is writing about our project and Dad's restaurant. This works.

Tristan finished his cake and headed for the door. "I'm spending tomorrow afternoon with my mother. Then she's leaving to go back to L.A., but we already have plans to be together at Thanksgiving. She promised to get those tiny chocolate turkeys we used to have as table decorations, when we were a real family." He paused. "Actually, those last words are mine. But I'm okay with all that. Dad will have me at Christmas. I think that's the way it's going to be. I'll be split in two every once in a while, but you know? I'll take it. It's better than feeling like half of me is always missing."

Chapter 42

An Unexpected Ending

Sam took his regular seat in the Monday morning biology lab, looking around for Ella. No sighting. He caught up with Matt and Tristan after second period, but still no Ella. "What's up with this?" he asked. "Have either of you heard from her?" They hadn't.

"But, yeah, I have some news," Tristan mumbled. "I overheard some kids in the hallway saying that Reed and the others got expelled. They cleaned out their lockers and everything else over the weekend."

Expelled: The word even *sounded* harsh. "Whoa. I didn't really expect that," said Matt. "I mean, maybe suspended. I would have thought some of their parents could have headed this off."

Sam shook his head. "The cheating that these guys did— over nine months? You've got to come down really hard on it. But yeah, expelled. It's so final. I wonder where they'll go from here."

It wasn't until early afternoon that he saw Ella walk into the building, head down, feet dragging, backpack hugged to her chest like it was the only thing keeping her upright. He ran to her, touched her hand, and led her to a bench outside.

He waited. She'll tell me, he said to himself. She's either dying or someone in her family has died, or their house burned down, or… But if any of that were true, she wouldn't be in school. So maybe someone in her family is just sick, not actually dead, or maybe their house was broken into, or her father had one too many crises at work and quit his job…. Or…

"I'm not dying," Ella finally said, looking up at him. "But I feel like I might as well be. We're moving, Sam. My father's company is transferring him, and we have to pack up and go in a month. I'm going to be put in a new school. They couldn't even wait for the semester to be over. I have to leave everything here, all my friends, my room, all the things I like doing, our bees… And you. I have to leave you. It doesn't seem fair that a person can just be ripped out of her home and taken to a new country that she didn't choose …"

"A new country?" Sam almost shouted. "You're going to a new *country*? What country?"

The family was moving to London. Ella's father had been asked to turn around the European operations of the fashion company that had just promoted him to head of international marketing. "They want him to start as soon as possible. My mother isn't thrilled, but she's already arranged it with her boss so that she can work from there and also scout around for new business opportunities. She'll be coming back to Manhattan every month or so. But basically we're done here. I'm done."

She began to cry very quietly—worse, Sam thought, than if she just out and out started bawling. He took both her hands. At this moment, he told himself, you have to be the one who looks ahead. Focus on the future. Figure it out. It won't be a separation. It will be … what? What will it be?

The bell for class rang. They stayed on the bench. Funny how things turn out, Sam thought. I wanted to win the contest, I wanted Dad's restaurant to succeed, I wanted the four of us to keep being friends and hanging out in New York and eating pastries and doing projects together. And I wanted to be with Ella for as long as I can imagine. Things had started to turn around. We won, Dad and I get to stay in New York ... and Ella is leaving. All my planning, and I never saw this coming.

He kissed the top of her head. His hand brushed up against the tears sliding down her cheek onto her sweater. "Ella, have you asked your parents if you could stay here, with a friend, or maybe with your cousins, and then spend vacations with them in London? It's not like you're in elementary school. And we would all look after you"—she smiled, probably for the first time that day, he thought— "not that you need looking after, except of course by me."

Ella had already floated those ideas and more—staying with friends, finishing eighth grade, finishing just the semester ... "I wanted to be here at least for the Washington trip. I did win that one. My mother will arrange it so that she and I can both be back in the U.S. for our celebration weekend. But that's it."

Another bell rang. "The funny thing is," Sam said, "I've kept so many secrets—my mother's death and how it almost ruined me and my Dad, their restaurant collapsing, the problems facing Bella Vista, the possibility that Dad could lose his job, the possibility that I could lose my scholarship. But my biggest secret was that you were the best thing, the only thing, that could have gotten me through the year. I mean I still think about my mom a lot, but she's a little blurrier now, a little out of focus, except when I dream. Then she seems so real, nearby, like I could wake up and find her in the kitchen making pancakes. And now you're leaving."

So, Sam thought, would I trade winning the competition for having Ella stay in Manhattan? Would I trade coming in last in the competition and losing my scholarship but having Ella stay? Dad once told me that we work with the hand we are dealt. It's wrong to think that everything will always go our way. It's just that I didn't expect this. I never expected this.

Had it really been more than eighteen months since his father had come home alone from the hospital with news that would upend their lives? Time, Sam decided, has a way of collapsing painful events into one long fluid memory that can only be distanced by another of life's somersaults—like a move to a new city, like the sudden entrance of a person whose smile could rock his world, a person who would be there, if not this month or this year, then another month, another year.

He and Ella went in just as the final class period of the day ended. They found Tristan and Matt and told them the news. Tristan looked at Sam. "I predict many plane trips to London," he said, "where the English people need a lot of help with the art of pastry making from expert American chefs."

Ella came close to a smile. "Tristan is a smart boy," she said. "We should always keep him on our team."

Matt looked hurt. "How can you leave, Ell? Everything is going so well for us. We're the invincible four, the heroes of the hour, the winners of the fight between good and evil, life and death..."

Ella gave him a hug. "We'll still be the invincible four. It's just that one of us may begin to develop an English accent. Think how much class that will add to our group."

Matt drew himself up and pulled his friends into a huddle. "I have an idea," he said. "What we need are some snacks while we figure out how to handle this latest crisis. Maybe we can find those hard-boiled eggs Ella likes and a few dozen brownies. Any suggestions? Sam, you haven't steered us wrong yet. How about if you lead the way."

Sam looked around at his friends. "The roof," he said, taking Ella's hand. "Back to where it all began."

END

AFTERWORD

"Bees on the Roof" tells the story of four seventh graders and their quest to win a science competition, but the real stars of this book are the tiny pollinators that play a crucial, and now threatened, role in our environment. While the following pages offer more information about honeybees and Colony Collapse Disorder, there is still much we don't know about these amazing insects. As Paul, the apiary center tour guide, notes at one point: If only bees could talk.

FUN FACTS ABOUT HONEYBEES

Speed and Distance: Foraging bees fly up to five miles on their nectar-gathering trips, traveling at a speed of between 15 and 20 miles per hour.

Honey by the Pound: To produce one pound of honey, foragers must cover approximately 55,000 miles and collect nectar from approximately one million flowers. Bees bought through the mail usually come in three-pound packages containing a separately caged queen. Each pound has about 3,000 to 4,000 bees.

The Queen: Queen bees can live up to five years, although their vigorous egg-laying duties often result in an earlier death. The queen's special diet of royal jelly is a secretion produced by young female bees that is made up of pollen and certain chemicals as well as dietary supplements, like Vitamin B. "Supersedure"—the replacement of a queen bee by her daughters – features "cuddle death," one of several rituals in which worker bees tightly surround the ailing queen until she dies from overheating. The same method is used to kill predatory wasps.

A Drone's Life: Drones are the product of unfertilized eggs; they do not have stingers, and they do not forage. They are there to mate with the queen, an activity that takes place about 200 to 300 feet in the air. A hive may contain anywhere from 20,000 to 80,000 female worker bees, but it typically houses, at most, several hundred drones. Their life span is approximately three months, whereas worker bees, who are the product of fertilized eggs, live about six weeks. Drones have bigger eyes than worker bees, the better to locate the queen bee in her aerial flight at mating time. A queen bee helps the process along by releasing pheromones—chemical substances—that alert the drones to her readiness for mating.

... And Death: Not all drones mate with the queen, but the ones that do face immediate death: Their internal mating apparatus is ripped out at the end of the encounter. Drones that don't mate are usually booted from the hive in late summer or early fall. By then, any usefulness they might have had is clearly over, and they are a drag on the hive's precious stores of nectar.

Food and Water: Sugar-rich nectar is the bees' main source of carbohydrates—the equivalent of our spaghetti and other pastas. Pollen provides protein. Bees, like us, always need water in their diet. They find it in such places as fountains, parks, stagnant puddles and damp rocks.

Pollination Nation: About one-third of our food supply comes from crops pollinated by insects. Bees, which do an estimated 80% of the work, fertilize almost 100 different fruits, vegetables, and nuts. The agriculture industry counts on bees to pollinate around $15 billion worth of crops each year. While honeybees are the main pollinators in our ecosystem, numerous others help out, including bumblebees and other varieties of native bees, hummingbirds, moths, wasps, butterflies, and bats. Also wind, rain, and people. Pollen can collect on our clothes and hands. When we move around in gardens and orchards, we deposit it on other plants.

The Hard-working Worker Bees: The first few weeks of a worker bee's life are spent as a "house bee" cleaning the hive, feeding the larvae and queen, and building wax comb. Towards the end of that time, she acts as a guard at the hive's entrance, sending out a special scent if she senses danger, such as a bear or wasp, to warn the other bees. The highest level a worker bee reaches is forager. Worker bees don't always die when they sting. If the target has a soft skin (humans have thick skins; some insects and reptiles don't), the stingers don't get stuck, and the bee can live to sting again.

Bees have two stomachs—one for digesting food, the other for storing nectar. And their sense of smell is much stronger than ours. Up to 170 odor receptors in their antennae help bees locate flowers, find their way home, and even detect disease in humans.

Dance Lesson: The waggle dance has been studied, viewed and dissected by many people in an effort to understand the complicated moves a forager makes to signal the location of her most recent nectar source. For example, the longer the bee waggles her tail, the farther away the location. By one estimate, for every 75 milliseconds a bee dances, the distance to the nectar is extended by another 330 feet. In terms of direction, if a bee dances in a direct vertical line to the sun, the nectar lies in that direction. But if she dances to the right (or left) of that vertical line by a certain number of degrees, then the nectar is located to the right (or left) of the sun at the exact same angle. Honeybees also do a "round dance"—moving in narrow circles—to indicate that the nectar source is close by, usually within 35 feet of the hive. The waggle dance points to nectar sources farther away.

Pollen and Your Health: Bee pollen, in capsule or granule form, is sold to the public in many forms—as a nutritional supplement, a way to lose weight, a method to stop premature aging, alleviate joint pain, cure skin rashes, staunch nosebleeds, or improve athletic ability, among other uses. Bee venom is promoted as a treatment for nerve pain and rheumatoid arthritis. Evidence for how well these remedies work is scant.

Busy Beeswax: Wax secreted by the bees as they make honeycomb is collected by beekeepers when they cut off the waxy caps of the honeycomb cells. We find beeswax in such products as lipsticks, shoe polish, crayons, and candles. Because beeswax can be easily cut, shaped, and mixed with other ingredients, it has been used since the Middle Ages to make death masks and statues of historic figures.

The Color of Honey: The color and flavor of honey depend on where the bee collects her nectar. "Clover" honey, an extra-light amber color with a sweet taste, comes from the clover plant. "Orange blossom" honey, a light amber color with a delicate, sweet citrus flavor, comes from orange trees in Florida and California. "Sourwood" honey, from the sourwood tree in the Appalachian Mountains, is not sour but sweet, with a hint of anise and spice. "Avocado" honey comes from avocado blossoms in California, has a dark color and a buttery or molasses taste, and contains more than the usual amount of minerals and vitamins. Blueberry honey, buckwheat honey, eucalyptus honey, and tupelo honey are examples of other varieties.

Honeybee History: According to some sources, the earliest evidence of a bee-like fossil dates back 100 million years to a site in Myanmar, while the first evidence of an actual honeybee fossil was found in Europe 35 million years ago. Ten-thousand-year-old depictions of honey harvesting have shown up at rock art sites in Spain and Africa, and honeybees were carved into the tombs of Egyptian pharaohs, including King Tutankhamun, also known as King Tut (14th century B.C.).

Bees were most likely brought to the U.S. from England in the early seventeenth century, appearing first in Virginia and later in New England. Thomas Jefferson reportedly called honeybees "white man's flies" and had a beekeeper and hives at Monticello, his plantation in Charlottesville, Virginia.

COLONY COLLAPSE DISORDER, AND WHY IT'S IMPORTANT

Colony Collapse Disorder remains the subject of continually evolving new theories. Some scientists now suggest that climate change could throw off pollination schedules because warmer weather affects where plants grow and when they bloom. Bees may not be primed to meet the needs of these new schedules. Scientists are also paying increasing attention to a group of insecticides called neonicotinoids (neonics, for short). The U.S. Environmental Protection Agency is looking into whether and how they disrupt bees' nervous systems. Neonics are manufactured by chemical companies and sold to farmers who use them to eradicate pests on cotton, citrus plants, wheat, and corn, among other crops. Chemical companies say the risk from neonics is overstated, and that they are necessary to protect our food supply.

Recent decisions by big agricultural producers to use all available soil for growing crops, thereby removing acres of land once filled with wildflowers and other sources of nutrition for bees, is cited as another potential contributor to CCD. Then there are the spooky "ZomBees," a term used to describe bees infected by parasitic "zombie flies." Eggs laid by zombie flies in a bee's abdomen hatch into larvae that eat away at the bee's brain and wings. Disoriented by these attacks, the bees begin to behave in odd and uncharacteristic ways. They leave their hives at night (which healthy bees rarely do), dance (not the waggle kind), and then fall to the ground, crawling around blindly in circles until they die.

Beekeepers in the U.S. lost approximately 33% of their honeybee colonies between April 2016 and April 2017, according to population surveys. This is an improvement over the 42% mortality rate of the previous year, but still represents an alarming number of honeybee deaths in this country. Some scientists, environmentalists, and organic beekeepers cite the dangers of a "toxic soup" of insecticides and herbicides used on farms and in fields as well as sprayed in hives to control mites, fungi, pests, and diseases. Chronic exposure to these chemicals, say opponents of pesticides, can make it difficult for bee colonies to breed and resist disease.

The number of managed honeybee colonies in the U.S. has decreased from 5 million in the 1940s to 2.89 million in 2017, according to the U.S. Department of Agriculture. The good news: 2.89 million represents a 3% increase over the previous year.

****

For more information on bees and "Bees on the Roof," visit Tumblehome Learning's website at http://tumblehomelearning.com/

ABOUT THE AUTHOR

Robbie Shell has spent most of her career as a business journalist. She got hooked on honeybees when she watched a video showing them walking in single file – no pushing or shoving, no butting in line – out of a square shoebox-sized container into a small hive in the middle of a garden full of wildflowers. The bees had two immediate goals: to begin setting up their new home and to start taking care of their queen. Teamwork, efficiency and dedication ruled.

Further research into honeybees explained how essential they are to our food supply, how amazing their communication and navigation systems are, and how seriously their existence is being threatened by Colony Collapse Disorder. Introducing honeybees to young people in a way that would highlight the crucial role these tiny insects play in our global environment seemed like a timely topic for a book.

A graduate of Princeton University, Robbie lives with her husband in Philadelphia. This is her first novel for young readers.

ACKNOWLEDGMENTS

Many people advised and encouraged me in the writing of this book. My brother Jamie Wyper, an architect and beekeeper, first introduced me to bees when he brought over a jar of honey from his hives. He was a steadfast supporter and reliable expert all the way through. My younger son Ned read the whole manuscript and caught errors that only a millennial would see. My older son Ben came up with the title, among other suggestions. My husband Richard provided invaluable marketing advice and kept saying, in so many words, "You can do this!" Seventh grader Trevor Russin offered such detailed and astute feedback that I am ready to sign him up to co-author my next novel. Paul Legrand, the beekeeper at Monticello, shared his vast knowledge of honeybees and took me on tours of the plantation's beautiful gardens. Children's author Libby Koponen offered early and crucial information on how to write for a middle grade audience. Glenn Ruffenach, a former editor of, and now contributor to, *The Wall Street Journal*, published an essay I wrote on honeybees and encouraged me to follow through on my idea for this book. Others who helped along the way include librarian and close friend Jan Westervelt, children's librarian Melanie Jacobs, science teacher Jennifer Hoffman, and my nephew Robby Wyper, whose love of nature was the inspiration for the book's main character. The following five people – bee experts and/or environmentalists—provided timely comments on earlier drafts: Mike Weilbacher, Jim Bobb, Debra Tomaszewski, Adam Schreiber, and Ellen Briggs. Finally, I would like to thank Tumblehome Learning's Penny Noyce, Barnas Monteith, and Yu-Yi Ling, who partnered with me on every aspect of the book's development, for their invaluable guidance and support.

ENDORSEMENTS

"*Sam and his friends discover that honeybees are incredibly cool animals, that nature is unbelievably interesting, and that the mysterious collapse of bee colonies worldwide is one of the most intriguing—and compelling—mysteries in science. As a naturalist, I like how Shell seamlessly weaves the science of bees and beekeeping into the plot, but I love how Sam and his friends discover a central truth: that nature heals, that connecting to nature makes us better people.*" — Mike Weilbacher, Executive Director, Schuylkill Center for Environmental Education, Philadelphia

"*Robbie Shell has done a fantastic job presenting information about honeybees and their struggles in an engaging way that kids can understand. Much like in a bee hive, the book's characters work together through thick and thin towards a common goal. They demonstrate that each person's actions can make a difference. This book will inspire and empower budding young environmentalists to stay involved in ecology issues. I love how it demonstrates that everyone can do their small part to help the planet, even if they live in an urban cityscape.*" — Debra Tomaszewski, Founder and Executive Director, Planet Bee Foundation

"*What a honey of a tale! Shell uses the world of teens — swarming with bullies, a science fair competition, friendship, loss, and first love — to teach readers about the crucial role of honeybees in our environment and a mysterious illness that is now threatening their very survival.*" — Jim Bobb, Chairman Emeritus, Eastern Apicultural Society of North America

"*A super fun and interesting story that is full of fascinating facts about honey bees and beekeeping! Readers will enjoy following the adventures of the 'Bee Team' as they embark on this journey of learning and discovery.*" — Adam Schreiber, former president of The Philadelphia Beekeepers Guild, backyard beekeeper and father to two budding beekeepers